ON NEPTUNE WINGS

All Will Cain ever wanted to be was a Navy Aviator. As incongruous as it seemed, his having been born and raised in Colorado and being instilled with a love for the mountains, he had a love for flying and for the sea. When he was sent to the Naval Air Station, in Brunswick, Maine and became a crewmember on an ASW (Anti-Submarine-Warfare) Navy Patrol aircraft, he knew he had found his life's work. Then he met Jamie Dunham, a local girl who lived in Brunswick with her family, and his life changed forever

On Neptune Wings

Jack Sprouse

A Black Opal Books Publication

GENRE: ROMANCE/COLD WAR

ON NEPTUNE WINGS
Copyright © 2019 by Jack Sprouse
Art Work Cheyenne Victoria Middleton, the Author's granddaughter
Cover photos used with permission
All cover art copyright ©2019
All Rights Reserved
Print ISBN: 9781644372326

First Publication: April 2020

Published by Black Opal Books **http://www.blackopalbooks.com**

DEDICATION

This book is dedicated to my best friend, Eddie Nettles, from New Orleans, Louisiana, who served with me in Vp-21 and remained my friend for 27 years until his death in 1989.

Eddie was the best man I ever knew.

There was a time, I tell you true

O'er furrowed fields of morning dew

On Neptune wings, I fairly flew

Through skies of iridescent blue

When I was twenty-one

CHAPTER 1

Will Cain sat in the forward observation station of a Lockheed P2V Neptune US Navy Patrol Aircraft, flying out of Guantanamo Bay, Cuba. with his binoculars held to his eyes, scanning the air and the sea, above, in front of and below the aircraft. A tiny speck appeared in the distance. It was barely visible even with the glasses.

Slowly the object drew closer as the plane approached. He could make out the form of a small boat or ship on the water but could see no flag or other markings. He clicked the button on his handset to notify the pilot.

"I've got a ship on the surface at nine o'clock low," he said. The pilot acknowledged and turned in that direction for a closer look.

"It's Cuban," Cain said, "I can see the flag."

It was a Cuban Navy Gunboat, not too unlike an American Coast Guard Cutter but not as large. Two double-barreled gun emplacements immediately began tracking the Neptune as it circled the little ship.

Cain swallowed hard and slid his seat all the way out into the Plexiglas bubble so he could better observe what was happening on the water below.

"This shit is real," he said out loud.

e⁄ɔe⁄ɔ

After A-School in Memphis, Will Cain received orders to report for duty with VP-21, an ASW (Anti- Submarine Warfare) squadron stationed at Brunswick Naval Air Station in Maine. Three days on a Greyhound bus brought him to the main gate facility on August 1, 1960 and a duty driver drove him to the VP-21 hangar.

"Where are the planes?" he asked the driver.

"The squadron is on deployment," the man said, "they'll be back in a week or two."

Will found the Duty Office on the second level of the hangar and knocked on the door. A voice from inside the office said, "come on in, it's open."

Will opened the door and stepped into the office. Behind the desk sat a Lieutenant JG who appeared to be busying himself with some paperwork on the desktop. "What can I do for you?" The man asked.

Will saluted then took off his hat. "Cain, William J reporting for duty, Sir," he said.

"Yes, I've been expecting you, I'm Lieutenant JG Kyle Murphy. I've been sent back with a small crew to get the facility ready for the rest of the squadron when they return from deployment, that should be any day now. I see you're an electrician. I can put you in charge of the electric shop. But first you need to go check into the barracks and get settled in. When you're finished come on back and I'll give you a tour of the hangar."

"How do I get to the Barracks?"

"I'll get our Duty Driver to take you. Check in with Ben Wattigney, it's spelled Wat-tig-ney but he says it Watney, so don't call him Wat-tig-ney. Ben is an AD 1, lifer, and a bit crusty but sometimes he's pretty congenial.

"Hey Martinez," the Lieutenant yelled, and a young man with green Airman Stripes on his sleeve came in from an adjoining room.

"Yes Sir, Mister Murphy," he said.

"This man is William Cain," he said, nodding toward Will. "He's a new man in the Electric Shop. He needs to go to the barracks and get checked in. Go with him and find Wattigney to get him situated."

"Yes, sir," Martinez said. "Come on, man, follow me. You go by William?"

"I go by Will usually but I'll answer to Cain. My dad is named William and he goes by Bill, go figure."

Martinez chuckled, "nobody goes by their real names around here. My name is Robert but I'm called Bobby, that's what my folks always called me. I'm from New Mexico, where are you from?"

"We're close, I'm from Colorado," Will replied, "Denver actually, born and raised."

"My family used to take me and my brothers to Pikes Peak in the summer, when I was a kid," Martinez said. "I've never been there in the winter though. I spent last winter here and that was no fun."

Will nodded. "It's not so bad in Colorado, as long as you're not in the mountains. It gets cold, of course but if the wind is not blowing and you're in a bright sun it can be thirty degrees and you'll be comfortable in a T-shirt. How bad does it get around these parts?"

"Pretty damned bad," he said. "You see how these barracks are built, with the covered walk connecting them? They form a courtyard between them and the wind blows the snow in and it piles up in drifts almost up to the second floor and the walkways are completely covered, it's like walking in a snow cave. So, it's best to bunk on the second floor so you don't get claustrophobia or something. It gets spooky on the first floor when you can't see out of the windows for the piled-up snow."

"I'll keep that in mind," Will said, "thanks for the info."

Ben Wattigney was, as Lieutenant Murphy had described him, loud and 'crusty' but with a degree of congeniality about him. He was constantly shouting orders to his crew of E-1 Recruits and E-2 Apprentices, directing them to sweep and clean the third floor or run the buffer on the second floor. Each man had a walkie-talkie which gave Ben instant contact with them. Every man had to be busy all the time, that was the Navy way, according to Ben Wattigney. He kept them running and working, busying himself with finding things for them to do.

Wattigney was nearing the end of his thirty years in the Navy and had been given the relatively cushy job of overseeing the cleaning and upkeep of the squadron living quarters. He normally had a crew of six or seven men but at this time he had been sent back from deployment with only four men to prepare for the squadron's return. He was about forty-eight or so, as best Will could figure (he was in fact only forty-five), the same age as Will's dad only much more haggard looking. Will assumed he drank a lot because his face was puffy and wrinkled.

He would learn later that Wattigney had joined the Navy at eighteen in 1933 and had been at NAS Kaneohe Bay in Hawaii, working and flying as a crewmember on Navy PBYs, when the Japanese attacked on December 7, 1941. He saw duty at various locations across the Pacific, as the United States pushed the Japanese Navy toward its homeland. Wattigney saw many of his aircraft destroyed by Japanese bombs. He still often voiced his hatred of the Japanese for blowing up his PBY and killing many of his friends at Kaneohe Bay the day the war started.

"So, you're fresh out of A School?" Wattigney asked Will.

"Yes Sir," Will responded.

"You don't have to call me Sir, Son. I'm not an

officer." Wattigney said.

"I'm sorry, I meant no offense."

The man got a laugh out of that. "Just call me Ben, all the guys call me Ben. I see you got your Crow, how did you manage that so fast?"

"I joined the Reserve when I was still in high school," Will said. "I went for aviation and made E-3 by the time I chose to go on active duty. I made E-4 right before I finished A School. I want to go on crew as soon as I can."

"Well good for you, Cain," Wattigney said. "You shouldn't have any problem doing that. Now, back to the business at hand, where do you want to bunk?"

"Bobby Martinez, the duty driver, said the second floor would be best because of the snow drifts in the winter. So, I guess I'll try the second floor."

"Second floor it is," he said and yelled for one of his men to take Will to the second floor and let him pick out a cubicle. He then went to his desk and retrieved a combination lock and gave it to Will for his locker.

The cubicles were equipped for four men but Wattigney's man informed him that only two men ever occupied one cubicle. Will picked out a cubicle near the bathroom and his escort left to get his sheets and blanket. He quickly returned with the bed gear and left Will alone to unpack his seabag and make his bed.

He walked back to the hangar and checked in with Lieutenant Murphy. The Lieutenant took him to the Electric Shop and gave him a list of the equipment that would be arriving on the transports. "The MATS (Military Air Transport Service) should be arriving with our gear tomorrow," Murphy told him. My hangar crew will bring all the containers into the hangar and it'll be up to you to get all the electrical stuff into your shop and storage bins. The forklift is available and I can get you some help if you need it."

"I'll be okay Mister Murphy. I can drive the forklift."

"Okay then, but don't hesitate to ask for a hand if you need it. We've got a lot of work to do before the troops come home."

"I won't," Will said, "thank you.

The packing crates were brought into the hangar and separated, as well as could be expected, by trades and by the various offices. Will found the boxes marked **Electric Shop** and began dragging them to the staging area in front of the space. He carried the tool boxes to the appropriate bins and the spare parts to theirs. Drawings and schematics were placed on the tables provided and other pieces of equipment were either filed or stored in the designated locations. He thoroughly cleaned the work spaces and tables and attached the locks Lieutenant Murphy had given him to the bins and doors to ensure that nothing disappeared. The Lieutenant told him to put the keys in the Duty Office key cabinet. In two days, he had the shop shipshape and everything cleaned, put away, and secured.

"Damn, Cain, you're not afraid of work, are you?" Lieutenant Murphy said. "You're the only one finished, these other guys are sloughing off a bit. Why don't you take the rest of the day off and go into town?"

Will had no vehicle so he asked where he could catch a bus into town. After changing into his civvies, he walked to the bus stop on the base and rode into town. Brunswick, Maine was a quaint town compared to Denver. People were not as friendly but Will would eventually learn that, once you got to know them, they weren't much different from people anywhere else. They talked funny, he noted, but he could understand them.

He had lunch at Clare's Grill and the food was good. The waitress, a woman named Betty according to her name tag, flirted with him and gave him free refills of his coke. "You just get into town?" she asked him.

Will nodded, "I'm in VP-21."

"The Black Jack Squadron," she said, "my ex-husband was in VP-23 but he didn't work out."

Will did not pursue the details of why the Former became the Ex.

Betty was about ten years older than he was, Will estimated, and not unattractive but not a real head-turner either. Her personality though was engaging so he talked with her without flirting back. "Where you from, Doll," she asked him.

"Colorado, Denver," he told her.

"I've always wanted to go to Colorado—just never got the chance. Maybe you can take me with you on your next Leave," she said, smiling at him.

"Why not? He said. "I'm sure my mom would like to meet you."

"Your mom, huh? Well at least you don't have a wife. How old are you, Sailor?"

"I'm nineteen," Will said.

"Oh shit, just my luck, I'm old enough to be your mother."

"No, you're not," he quickly responded, you can't be that old."

"I'm thirty-five, young man."

Well you certainly don't look that old, "I would have figured you for around twenty-nine or so."

"Oh, thanks, I appreciate that," she said, "you're quite a charmer. Just watch out for these local girls, they're always looking to marry a Navy man so they can get the hell out of here."

"Why?" He asked. "This seems like a pretty nice place to live. I'm going to be here a while so I better like it."

"I guess it's as good as anyplace if you're from here. I was born and raised here so I don't know any better."

"Well thanks for the advice, I'll be on guard lest some

local girl tries to marry me when I'm not looking."

She laughed and handed him his check. "Come back in anytime you're in town," she said.

"I will, Betty, thanks," he told her, then paid the cashier and left.

MATS planes arrived with the squadron personnel on the fifth of August and the aircraft flew in the next day. Will was in the Electric Shop when a big Chief Petty Officer walked in. Chief Raymond (Ray) Purcell was a big man, at least six feet four and starting to plump up a bit. Purcell was a loud man with little regard for social graces. "Who are you?" he addressed to Will.

Cain, William J, Chief. I've been assigned to the Electric Shop. I'm an AE-3 just out of A School," Will replied.

"I can see that," the Chief responded. "Are you the man who put everything in order here?"

"Yes Sir, Chief," Will told him. "I think I've got everything in place. If you can't find something just let me know, I made an inventory list of where I stored things.

"Good work," the Chief said, "thank you. Some of the men will be going on leave since they've been gone five months so I'm happy to have the extra help. We'll resume operations right away and most of the planes will need scheduled inspections."

"Okay, Chief, just tell me what you want me to do."

"You can work with John Dolinski, he's my lead man. Ski will get the schedules and bitch lists and show you what to do."

When Will returned to the barracks after work the place was filled with the new residents. In his own cubicle, he encountered a red-haired lanky kid with a boyish face unpacking his seabag. "Oh, hey guy, how you doin'?" he asked, and extended his hand. "I'm Jimmy Watson."

Will shook his hand, "Cain, Will Cain," he said. "Glad to meet you. Welcome to the cube."

"Thanks," Jimmy said. "I wanted to be close to the shitter, I hope you don't mind."

"No, not at all, that's why I picked this cube. What do you do in the Squadron?"

"I'm a Tron, Radioman on LH 12. You're a Sparky I see, you goin' on crew?"

"I hope to," Will said. But right now, I'm just working in the Electric Shop."

"So, you met Ski, Dolinski I mean? He's a good guy, one of the best, I hear from the other guys."

"Yeah, yeah, I worked with him a couple of days," Will said. "He sure seems to know a lot. He went over the schematics with me and showed me how to troubleshoot a little. I've got a lot to learn. Until I got here, I'd only been to A School so I don't have much hands-on experience."

"It just takes time and effort, like anything else I guess," Jimmy said. "Hey, I got to go meet my buddy Andy, he's the second Mech. On my crew. We're going into town, I'll catch up with you later."

"Okay, Will said and nodded, nice talking to you."

Jimmy hustled out of the cube and ran down the corridor to the exit door.

The Squadron had resumed full operation status and there were typically two aircraft at a time in the hangar undergoing maintenance. The Neptune was not a beautiful airplane, it was sort of cumbersome looking, but it was an interesting aircraft, and rather unique in appearance Will thought. The forward observation station, called 'The Bubble' by most crewmembers was a Plexiglas covered compartment with a chair on rails. The chair could slide back and forth all the way up to the front of the space and back out to permit exit from the chair and the compartment. Access was gained by climbing a ladder located on the aft bulkhead of the nose wheel well. A hatch, immediately above the entry ladder, permitted entry to the flight deck and the rest of the aircraft. The flight deck, just aft of the Cockpit, housed the electronic equipment along the starboard side of the aircraft on a shelf where the AT's (Electronic Technicians) sat to operate the gear.

The radar equipment was located in a compartment called the Radome, just behind the nose wheel well. A small hatch door permitted entry into the space. There was also a hatch in the floor of the aft fuselage near the sono-buoy chutes. On either side of the aircraft were two windows for observers who sat in chairs provided for that purpose. The windows could be lifted up and snapped into retainers on the inside of the fuselage. Men would often rest their arms on the edge of the opening much like riding in a car. From these locations, and from the forward observation station, the camera crews operated.

Although searching for submarines and surface warships was the primary mission of the Neptune crews much of the flight time was spent in surveillance of commercial shipping. This involved photographing each ship, determining its name, plotting its position, course and speed, and noting significant information about any visible cargo and whether it was loaded or in ballast. The squadron was also involved in monitoring and filming the fleets of Russian Trawlers off the east coast of the United States and shot some of the clips seen in a 'Twentieth Century' program called 'Red Ships off our Shores'.

The protrusion on the back of the aircraft housed the MAD (Magnetic Anomaly Detector) gear. This instrumentation was used to detect minute variations in the Earth's magnetic field. A mass of ferromagnetic material, like a submarine, creates a detectable disturbance in magnetic field and locates the target via signals transmitted from a sonobuoy dropped into the sea from chutes in the back of the aircraft.

Will spent the next few months working in the Electric Shop, doing routine hour inspections on the various aircrafts, and replacing parts. The worst part was working on a plane outside in the cold. Many times, the ground crews had to clear a path through the snow just to get to the plane. It was brutally cold and impossible to work on an airplane with gloves on. A man would have to warm his hands in his pocket for a few minutes and then turn screws and nuts & bolts to remove a part and then replace it. It was an arduous process. Their fingers would get so cold they would sting mightily.

Will stayed after working hours to study the schematics (wiring diagrams) to learn more about how the various systems operated. They had taught him to read schematics at A School but his education had not been specific to the Neptune and he found it fascinating to trace the wiring systems through the numerous compartments. Each wire in a system had its own number, usually a six or seven-digit number that appeared at every termination of the wire in the specific system.

One who was adept at reading schematics could look at a particular item, such as a relay, and see which position it should be in when a given condition is known. If a relay is supposed to be in the open position when a particular piece of equipment, such as the landing gear, is up then he can simulate that condition by manipulating a microswitch that indicates that condition, then check the relay with a multimeter such as the TS297/U and determine if the device is working properly. A single relay may cause several actions to take place at once. One set of contacts may control indicator lights and another set on the same relay may turn on an equipment cooling fan for another system.

LH-12 was in the hangar for some regular maintenance and with a few discrepancies, or items on the bitch-list as they were called. Chief Purcell told Will to check out the pilot's complaint about the G2 compass and Will took the drawings with him into the aircraft. He first determined that the equipment had no power supply, so he was tracing the circuitry back to the equipment rack in the back compartment of the plane. An inspection of the black box that controlled the equipment revealed a loose cannon plug on the back. The plug had apparently vibrated loose, and the pin connection had been broken, preventing power from going to the unit. Will tightened the plug and safety-wired it then turned the equipment on and found that it was working properly.

As he exited the aircraft an officer approached him. "I'm Lieutenant Powell," the man said. "This is my airplane. You're the electrician, right?"

"Yes Sir, Mister Powell, Cain is my name."

"Alright, Cain, it's nice to meet you." Will nodded. "Can you check out my G2 compass?" Powell asked him. "It wasn't working when we flew in last night."

"I fixed it," Will said, "a cannon plug had come loose and the unit was not getting power."

"Show me, if you don't mind," the Lieutenant said.

Will showed him the equipment and the guilty plug. "I tightened it and safety-wired it. It's working now."

"What the hell would have caused that?" Powell said.

"I don't know, Sir. Maybe the last time they replaced the black box they didn't tighten it all the way."

"Did they not safety-wire it either?" he asked, visibly concerned.

Will realized that he had to be careful what he said. All maintenance on the airplanes was documented so a record of when the equipment was last checked would be available for review. He knew he could be getting someone in hot water but at the same time he wanted to shoot straight with the officer. "I will let Chief Purcell know about this and I also wrote it on the discrepancy log," Will said.

"Thanks, Cain," Powell told him. "I appreciate your fixing it."

"No problem, Sir," Will Replied and saluted. "Nice to meet you."

Powell returned the salute. "You too," he said.

Will told the Chief about his repairing the compass and passed on his conversation with the Lieutenant. Purcell was not pleased.

"That lazy fuckin' Harris," he blurted out. "He's fucked up one too many times now. I'm going to write his ass up for this."

Will learned that Frank Harris was the electrician on LH-12, Lieutenant Powell's airplane. Harris was the same rank and rating as Will. His negligence in failing to properly connect the equipment, was only a minor inconvenience to the pilot on this occasion. But it could have been more serious, had it been a critical system on which he had been working. Chief Purcell did not get to be head of the Electric shop by being everyone's friend and he did write up Harris, an act that resulted in Harris being grounded for a month.

"Get your head out of your ass, Frank," Will heard the Chief yell at Harris, "or I'll pull you off crew."

Harris offered no excuses for his mistake, only an apology nor did he fault Will for finding it. Cain was only following procedure and was just doing his job. But Harris was given to laziness. He'd been in the Navy for eight years and in VP-21 for three of those years. This was not the first time he'd 'screwed up' and whether he would remain on flight crew status was up to Lieutenant Powel.

One Friday afternoon, after work, Will was sitting on his bunk writing a letter to his folks when Sam Kinney, First Mech. On LH-12, walked in. "You seen Egg Money?" He asked Will.

"I don't know what that is." Will replied.

"Egg Money…Jimmy Watson, my Radioman." Kinney said.

"Oh, Jimmy's in the Head."

Kinney left and returned a few minutes later with the aforementioned Radioman, Jimmy Watson. Watson quickly dressed While Sam Kinney waited impatiently. "Hey Will," Jimmy said, "you want to go into town with us? We're going to have a few beers and maybe go over to Lewiston and look for girls."

Will thought for a moment and Sam Kinney motioned

with his head. "Yeah Will, come on with us," he said. You've been working way too hard from what I hear, you could use some diversion."

Will consented and changed into his civilian clothes. They all got into Kinney's '56 black and yellow Chevy and headed off the base. "I have to pick up some cleaning at J & J," Kinney said.

"Sam only comes here because he's in love with the girl who works the counter," Jimmy confided to Will as they pulled into the parking lot of the Cleaners. "He thinks she's Miss America but I think she's too skinny."

"She's not skinny," Sam retorted. "She's perfect."

"She's got no tits." Jimmy said, with resignation.

"She has tits, Will, don't listen to him." Sam responded. "Egg Money likes fat girls."

"I've been meaning to ask why you call Jimmy Egg Money." Will said. "Why 'do' you call him Egg Money?"

"I gave him that name," Sam said. "Jimmy met a farm girl at the Farmer's Market in Brunswick. She was bringing her dad's eggs in to sell them. Her dad apparently lets her keep the money from her sale of the eggs, sort of like an allowance I guess. Well it seems that Brunhilda…

"Patty," Jimmy interjected. "Her name is Patty, not Brunhilda."

"Oh, right, Patty, I'm sorry Jimmy," Sam said. "So, Patty spotted Jimmy Watson and was smitten. She took him to lunch with the money she made off the eggs, and she takes him out every time she comes into town with the cackle berries."

"Hence the term, Egg Money," Will said, "I get it."

"Exactly," Sam said. "And that's how Jimmy got his war name."

The girl running the cash register at J & J Cleaners seemed not to notice the three Navy men as they entered the shop. She didn't look up until Sam Kinney approached the counter with his ticket. She took the ticket and went to retrieve his clothes, hung them on the hangar by the register, and rang up his bill. "That will be Two dollars and seventy-five cents," she told him.

"How about dinner and a movie tomorrow night Jamie?" he asked her. She shook her head.

"I've told you Sam my dad doesn't let me date Navy guys."

"But you're eighteen," he said. "Aren't you old enough to decide for yourself now?"

"I still live at home so I respect his wishes," she told him. She glanced up at Will and her eyes caught his. Something happened that he did not try to comprehend at the time and something on which he would not speculate, but he felt a fluttering sensation in his stomach near his solar plexus as her eyes smiled at him. He was just a little embarrassed because it was noticeable to Sam and Jimmy. Jimmy smiled broadly and Sam almost groaned.

"She likes Will," Jimmy said after they were back in the car.

"Remind me not to bring you with me next time," Sam responded. "I've been trying to get her to go out with me for almost a year now and you walk in one time and she's smiling at you and don't know I'm alive."

"Women are flighty, she probably just did that to make you jealous," Will told him, but he knew better. Perhaps he was projecting his own feelings onto the girl's and assuming she'd had the same sensation he did, but he didn't think so. There had been a connection between them he was convinced, when their eyes met. Sam was right, she was a pretty girl, one that many men would consider beautiful. One taken with her, as was Sam Kinney, would certainly have described her as beautiful. She had shoulder length blonde hair and strangely smoky blue eyes. Her build, not skinny but almost skinny, was slender and Will figured her to be about 5' 4" and appeared to be very de-mure and vulnerable, but the confidence she displayed in dealing with Sam belied that notion.

"I know where Will is going to be bringing his cleaning from now on," Jimmy said, to Sam's chagrin. Will brushed aside the comment and said nothing.

ॐॐॐ

By December the snow was piled up on the median along Maine Street so high that you could not see the buildings on the other side. Even for one accustomed to heavy snow it was a surprise. He'd seen two feet of snow regularly in Denver but they didn't usually leave it piled up like that. They often had to get plows to clear a path out to the airplanes on the ramp so they could get to them to work or for the flight crews to prepare them for a mission. Will had seen such snow accumulation in the mountains but 'down on the ground' as he referred to the eastern plain, it was a rare occurrence.

Will applied for two weeks Christmas leave and it was approved so he planned to go home for the holidays. He flew out of Portland, changed planes in Chicago, and ar-rived at Stapleton Airport to find his mom and dad waiting for him. He cut a handsome figure in his Dress Blues and White Hat, his mother told him. She cried as he hugged her. His dad shook his hand and then hugged him. "You look sharp, Son. He said. How're they treating you?"

"Good, Dad, I'm working in the Electric shop and learning a lot. I haven't applied to get on crew yet but I intend to. Where are Tommy and Julie?"

"They're getting the house ready for you," his mother said.

The drive to the Cain home in Lakewood took about forty-five minutes and when they got there, Will saw a

huge banner across the front of the house that read WEL-
COME HOME WILL. Some of the neighbors were brav-
ing the cold, and standing on the front porch with Will's
brother and sister, to greet him. He was a little uncomfortable with all the attention but he acted pleased. For their
benefit, and greeted, hugged and shook hands and thanked
everyone for being there.

Bill and Ellen Cain had three children, the oldest they
named William after his father. They called him Will to
avoid any confusion in addressing father and son. A girl
they named Julie, after Ellen Cain's mother, followed two
years later and a second son two years after that. The Cains
were a close family. Both parents had planned greater
things for their eldest son than a hitch in the Navy. They
had wanted him to go to college, Colorado University pref-
erably, but Will had other ideas. The boy was filled with
Wanderlust from the time he first started walking. When
he got older he often borrowed his dad's pickup truck and
went off into the mountains for two days at a time, sleeping
in the bed of the truck with his rifle and his Labrador re-
triever he called Boxer.

His folks had kept his room for him, just as he'd left it,
and it felt good to be sleeping in familiar surroundings.
The military life was unstable by its very nature. He was
subject to deployment at just about any time. Everything
he owned in life could be packed into his seabag and one
additional suitcase he kept for his civilian clothes. Patrol
Squadron Sailors rarely wore their uniforms "on the
beach" meaning off base. One would travel in uniform
when on Leave because commercial airlines offered free
airfare on standby status, depending on availability, if the
man wore his uniform.

Will loved being home for short periods of time to see
his folks and his siblings, but he carried the feeling with
him that he would probably never come back to live here

permanently. He asked his dad for a loan to buy a car to take back with him to Maine. "I have about a thousand dollars saved up but I want a new car. A used one might break down. If you can loan me the rest, I'll make regular payments," he said.

"Let's finance the car in your name and I'll co-sign for you," Bill Cain suggested. "That way it will help you build up a good credit rating."

"Thanks Dad, I appreciate it." Will said.

Bill Cain was 44 years old and graying a bit around the temples. He was at a time in his life when his appearance was starting to change. He was no longer a robust young man but was not yet old enough to be considered 'over the hill.' The graying hair gave him a distinguished look and he had kept his slender build so Will's father was not a homely man. Having started a hardware store when Will was still a baby, and expanding that store into a chain of stores across Colorado, the Cains were fairly well off. He could easily have bought his son a new car right out, as a gift but he sought to give Will the opportunity and the responsibility to pay for the car himself. Will agreed with the sentiment and did appreciate his father's help.

He found a blue 1961 Ford Falcon he liked. The price was $2,100. Will put up $800 for a down payment, and kept the extra money for his trip back. He would make 24 payments of $75 each which included the interest on the loan. He would now be independent and not have to rely on the other guys for a ride into town. His horizons had suddenly expanded. Buying the car meant that he had to leave home three days early in order to get back before his Leave was up. He was back in Brunswick on the third of January.

The car was a big hit with the guys in the squadron. Sam Kinney smiled devilishly and nodded his head up and down and told him "I know what you're doing, Will, don't try to put no shit past me. You got that car because of the girl at the cleaners, didn't you?

Will started shaking his head but Sam would not have it. "Come on now," he said, wagging his finger, "you can't bullshit a bullshitter. You ought to know that by now."

Will smiled slightly, knowing that Sam was probably right. He had been thinking about Jamie, even remembered her name, and he knew that the car would at least improve his chances of meeting her.

"Ha, I was right, you're going to try and take my girl away from me, ain't you?"

Jimmy Watson was listening and joined in the ribbing. "That girl don't even know you exist, Sam. I see the way she looks at Will. You're wasting your time. You been wasting your time for a year now, taking clothes in to get cleaned, hell, you even took some clothes in once that was already clean."

Sam laughed and nodded his head in agreement with Jimmy's conclusion.

"Don't feel too bad, Sam," Will said. "I'll tell her what a great guy she passed up. She'll regret letting you get away from her, one day."

Jimmy laughed and Sam just said, "aw bullshit."

While Frank Harris was grounded, Lt. Powell requested that Will be assigned to his crew to a temporary basis to fill in for his errant electrician. Chief Purcell was reluctant at first. He had come to consider Will one of his best troubleshooters but he didn't want to hold the boy back from advancing his career so he consented to Powell's request. Will would be a standby crewmember and would draw flight pay. The only condition was that he log at least 4 hours a month in the air. This was not a difficult requirement since most patrols lasted 10 hours or longer.

"Do you know how to operate the ECM gear, Cain?" Powell asked him."

"Yes Sir," Will replied, I learned it in A School."

"Good, if I need you on that I'll let you know, but for now you can ride in the bubble and keep me apprised of anything you see, on the water or in the air. Got that?"

"Yes Sir," Will said "got it."

His first flight came about a week later when the crew was assigned to what Jimmy Watson called a 'Bravo Sierra' mission. Will made the mistake of referring to the flight as a 'Bravo Sierra' in earshot of Lt. Powell and Powell asked him where he heard the term. "Watson told me that was the designation for this mission, Mister Powell." Will said.

"Egg Money, I'm not surprised. These guys are going to mess with you until you earn your place here, Cain. Don't pay too much attention to them. Bravo Sierra means bullshit. That's just Watson's way of tweaking the nose of authority."

"I'm sorry, I thought he was serious."

"His nickname is Egg Money. Do you expect a man with that name to be serious?"

"I guess not," Will said, smiling, "thank you Sir."

Will climbed the ladder up into the nose wheel well and crawled into the forward observation station, the bubble it was called by most of the crewmembers. He sat himself down in the chair and slid it in and out to make sure it was working properly. The aircraft started lumbering out to the runway and turned to the left when it reached the takeoff point. Will had only flown on commercial airplanes up to this point and he expected them to take off right away but they stopped for a short while and then the pilot ran up the engines to full throttle. The plane shook dramatically and Will was afraid that one of the engines might blow a gasket, but neither of them did as they started rolling down the runway. The excitement was almost more than he could bear. He felt full, full of life and full of himself. Here he was at nineteen and the Navy trusted him with the most important job on the airplane, if you didn't count the pilot that is. He was responsible for informing the aircraft commander of any threat to the airplane from above or below. In his mind, it was a critical service he had to perform. He knew this would all sound silly to someone else, if he told them what he was thinking, but that was how this experience made him feel.

They reached the roll point and the nose of the plane lifted off the runway and climbed into the sky. Below, the snow-covered landscape rushed by at an ever-increasing speed as Will observed farmhouses and highways and dozens of inlets along the rocky coast of the state of Maine. Then they were out over the Atlantic and the airplane seemed to quit trying so hard and settled down into cruising speed. They would fly to a predetermined point to begin their wide area patrol. Basically, they would fly around in a circle for ten hours or so and Will would keep them safe from harm. After four hours in the air he had not spotted so much as a seagull and Will was starting to understand why he was assigned this duty.

It had been dark for about an hour when Lt. Powell informed him that he could leave his post and come to the back of the plane to get some food and take a nap, if he were so inclined. Will climbed up to the flight deck and crawled over the wing beam and stopped to talk to Jimmy Watson in the radio compartment for a few minutes, then went to the back of the plane to find a spot to lie down. He was awakened by Andy Malik, the Second Mech. on the crew, telling him they were about to land.

"We're back home," Malik told him. "Did you have fun?"

"It was more exciting than I expected," Will said, smiling, and Malik laughed.

"It gets better, Will, these ASW patrols can be boring

as hell, but we do a lot of surface ship reconnaissance and that really is fun. I run the cameras sometimes and the guy in the bubble has a lot more to do. Besides, we take a lot of road trips to far off exotic places. Word is you'll be on crew soon, you'll get to love it."

"I actually loved it," Will said. "Yeah, it was boring but it was such a rush. Being all alone up there in the bubble was almost like a religious experience. I can't wait until I get to go again."

Andy smiled knowingly. "I had the same feeling the first time I went up. Like I said, word is that you'll be going with us again soon. Mister Powell likes you and I'm hearing that Frank may be taken off crew and odds are that you'll replace him."

"Are you serious, Andy?"

"I am," he said. "Chief Purcell says you're his best troubleshooter, except for Ski, and Lieutenant Powell has taken a liking to you. Frank Harris is a nice enough fella' but he's a drunk and he's lazy. He may have shit in his Dixie Cup one too many times." Dixie cup was vernacular for a sailor's white hat, his regulation head wear.

"I don't wish him any trouble but I do want to go on crew. I hate for it to be at his expense."

"Don't worry about it, Will," Andy said. "If it happens it happens, it won't be your fault he fucked up."

Andy Malik had been born and raised in Lewiston, Maine. It was by a quirk of fate that he had drawn NAS, Brunswick as a duty station so he was close to home and usually spent at least one weekend a month with his folks. That was all he could take, he explained. He knew the Lewiston-Auburn area and knew a lot of girls from high school so Andy was popular with the other members of his crew. Andy had no car so Sam Kinney would often drive him to his parent's house in Lewiston and his Dad would bring him back to the base.

Will started hanging out with Jimmy Watson and Sam Kinney and they usually went places in Sam's car, but since Will came back from Christmas Leave with a new car, he had become their go to guy. They started treating him like a member of the crew even though it had not yet been made official. Will was too young to drink so he was the logical duty driver. Andy was also too young to drink but he had a fake driver's license. It was not actually a fake license but rather an old license he'd gotten, and altered to appear current, from an older cousin who lived up-state somewhere.

Andy was a handsome man but the license contained a picture of his cousin, who was not a handsome man. This often, brought comments from bartenders and bouncers who checked IDs at the door of the bars they frequented. Most just overlooked the obvious fake ID and let him drink. Only on a couple of occasions was he refused to be served beer. The drinking age in Maine was 21 but most folks believed that, if a man could serve in the military, he ought to be allowed to drink.

This Saturday it was Will's turn to drive. The four of them got into his Ford Falcon and they drove into town. The snow was high in the middle of Maine Street and at one street corner someone or something walked out into the street right in front of the car. Will hit the brakes and yelled, "ah shit, what was that?"

"What was what," Jimmy said.

"Somebody walked in front of my car."

"I don't see anything."

Then Will noticed two hands on his hood. Apparently, someone was trying to pull himself up from the street. The person stood up and banged on the hood of the car with his fist then walked on across the street. "There he is," Will said.

"That's Fred," Andy yelled. "He's a fuckin' midget,"

and rolled down his passenger side window. "Hey Fred, get your midget ass out of the road. You wanna get killed?"

The little man turned and scowled back at the car. "Fuck you, assholes," he said. "I have the right of way here."

"Damn, I could have killed him," Will said. "Who is that guy?"

"Fred has dual roles in Brunswick Town society," Jimmy explained. "He's the town midget and also the town drunk, saves the city fathers the trouble of having to designate two positions. Fred always drinks for free, everybody buys him drinks just because he's Fred."

They spent the day at the home of Andy's parents. Andy's mom made dinner for them and a few of Andy's friends from the neighborhood, girls he knew, came over to mingle with him and his buddies from the base. Nearby there was a pretty good-sized hill that was covered with snow.

Andy's girlfriend was Jeanie Randall and she brought two friends with her to meet Andy's friends from the base, they were Bobbie Reynolds and Elaine Meador. Bobbie was not a pretty girl but, as the Navy men often described homely women, "had a great personality." Sam Kinney, who fancied himself a 'Ladies' Man' took an immediate shine to Elaine Meador. Elaine was very pretty with shoulder-length brown hair and all the accoutrements a man could want in a woman. "Is there anything I can do for you, beautiful?" he asked her.

Elaine brushed right past him and approached Will. "You can introduce me to your friend here," She said.

"Aw crap, Will," Sam said, being very animated and displaying mock frustration. "Did the Navy send you to VP-21 just to ruin my life?" They all laughed at that and Bobbie Reynolds went over to him and took his arm.

"You can do something for me," she told him. "You can go snow disking with me."

"Well hell, come on Girl, I can't dance so I might as well die in the snow or up against a tree."

The snow disk, or saucer, was a common item in Maine, along with sleds and toboggans. It was a round metal or plastic bowl on which usually only one person would sit and ride down a hill trying to avoid hitting a tree or falling off. But often two people would crunch together, always a guy and a girl, and ride the devious thing. It afforded the opportunity for a guy to get very close to a girl. The girl would hold on to the disk and the guy would hold on to the girl, pulling her up against him very tightly.

Elaine took Will by the arm of his coat, as they ascended the hill, and told him. "You're with me, you have any problem with that?"

"No," Will said, matter of factly.

"Well you sure have a way with words," she said. "Maybe I should do all the talking."

"Okay," he said.

"Do you ever say more than one word at a time?" She asked him. "Or is this just your bashful boy routine?"

"I do, on occasion," he told her. "I just was not expecting to meet the prettiest girl in the state of Maine tonight."

"Oh, a bullshit artist," she replied. "Are all you navy guys full of shit?

"No, I mean I don't know, but I'm not. I was being honest. You're the prettiest girl I've seen since I came here," he lied. "Okay, let me start over. I'm not declaring that you are the prettiest girl in the state, I'm just saying you're the prettiest girl I've seen so far. There may be lots of girls prettier than you in the State of Maine, I'm sure there are—" He paused a moment. "—or maybe not."

She was laughing. "I was right. You're all full of bullshit."

Will was unaccustomed to the use of profanity by girls. It just did not happen in the world in which he grew up. Profanity was not permitted in his household at home. But this girl used it loosely and freely. He learned later that Elaine had three brothers and that was undoubtedly where she acquired the habit, or vice as the preference might be. But gosh, she was good looking and he was just hoping he could keep from making a fool of himself.

"Okay, here's how it works, navy guy, you sit down on the disk first and I'll get in your lap, Okay"

"Okay," he said, and did as she ordered. They pushed off and started flying down the hill. He'd owned a sled back home but had never even seen a snow disk before today. He had no idea they could go so fast. Elaine was guiding the thing and appeared to know how to avoid hitting something hard, like a tree or a rock. They weaved into and around the trees at the bottom, Will just held on to her.

Elaine squealed as they tumbled over and landed in a pile of snow. She pulled him close to her and kissed him, a long embracing kiss which he happily returned. "Did you enjoy the ride, Will?" She asked him.

"Almost as much as that kiss," he said.

"You were getting a boner, weren't you?"

"I don't know." Will replied. "I was too busy trying to stay on that thing to think about anything else."

"Trust me," she said. "I know a boner when I feel one."

"Well, I'm not surprised, when you've got the prettiest girl in the State of Maine on your lap..."

"Yeah, yeah, I know. I've heard that before."

"I'm not surprised at that either," he said.

They made at least ten more trips down the hill and each one ended with the two of them in a lover's embrace kissing. Each time it grew more intense. Will knew he was going to go to bed with this girl at some point in the near future. He was incredulous at his good fortune. She just seemed to have fallen for him that quickly. There had to be something wrong with her, he told himself. Andy confirmed his suspicions on the ride back to the base.

"She's a little nutty, Will," he said. "Jeanie says that Elaine is 'in love with love', whatever the hell that means. Not trying to minimize your good looks and charm but Elaine falls in love very easy and gets very possessive after a while. I dicked her a couple of times, and it was well worth the trouble but Jeanie doesn't know so don't say anything. If I were you, I'd just ride her until she gets to be too much trouble and then dump her."

"I don't know if it'll go that far or not," Will said.

Oh, it'll go that far," Andy said. "Believe me Will, there is no way in hell you are going to get out of dicking Elaine Meador…unless you go AWOL tomorrow and don't ever come back to Maine."

"I didn't mean to say I wanted to get out of it," Will started to say as they all burst into laughter.

Will made three more flights with LH-12, two of which were ASW patrols and one of which was surface surveillance. Will spotted a boat on the water on the first mission and made his first actual report. "Object on surface, 9 o'clock." Lieutenant Powell acknowledged and turned to check it out. The boat turned out to be a local fishing boat. The people on board waved at the plane and Will waved back at them. On the third mission, they tracked some Russian trawlers and took pictures of them. Andy Malik requested permission to throw the trash out of the aircraft onto the trawlers but was denied. Some crews had done that in the past but it was not a generally acceptable practice.

Shortly after New Year's Day, 1961, Frank Harris showed up for work with alcohol on his breath and was written up by Chief Purcell and, after standing for a

Captain's Mast, was reduced in rate and kicked off crew.

Will Cain became the new electrician on the LH-12 crew. Sam, Andy, and Egg Money took him out drinking in celebration. Will got drunk for the first time since he'd been in high school

CHAPTER 2

Jamie

February 1961, was harsh in the state of Maine. At the beginning of the month the snow drifts were still covering the first-floor windows and Will was glad he'd taken the advice Bobby Martinez had given him about bunking on the second floor. At least they had sunlight when it was available. But the temperatures began to rise over the course of the month and the snow slowly began to melt. By April they were in the 50's and it was becoming quite pleasant.

Elaine Meador had turned out to be both a blessing and a curse. Elaine had "made a Vee," as Andy Malik put it, very easily in his car the first time they went out. Will had begun to think he was just being used as a sex object. He chuckled when he thought that, he imagined it sounded like something a girl would say but the truth was that he had hoped that Andy was either lying or just wrong about Elaine. It would be nice to have a girl he could talk to and who would talk back. He quickly came to realize that Elaine was not that girl. The sex was good but he guessed that, after all, he was just an old-fashioned boy who wanted more out of a relationship.

He spent a weekend at Elaine's house when her parents were out of town. It was awkward that Elaine didn't seem the least bit bothered by the prying eyes of the Meador family neighbors. Will felt their eyes on him every time they left the house. He worried that one of them would tell Elaine's parents but apparently, none did because nothing was ever said to him about it. According to Andy, The Meadors had problems of their own. Elaine was not the paradigm of virtue most parents wanted their daughters to be but they had pretty much given up on that expectation of theirs.

Their relationship simply died of natural causes when Will stopped going to see her. It was that easy. Egg Money offered him some advice. "Don't give in and call her the first time you get horny," he said. And Will didn't, although it had crossed his mind a couple of times. He couldn't stop thinking about the girl at the Cleaners in town and he began plotting how he could see her again without being as obvious as taking his clothes in for cleaning. She seemed smart enough to see through that.

He began having lunch at Clare's Grill on occasion, mainly because it was just up the street from the Cleaners where the girl worked. The food was good and he enjoyed talking to Betty the waitress who was entertaining and made him feel good about himself because she was always telling him he was good looking.

"I went home on Leave a while back," Will told her.

"Did you tell your mother about me?" Betty asked, smiling slyly at him.

"The subject didn't come up. I think she was afraid to ask if I'd taken up with a good-looking older woman."

"Well now, look at you." Betty responded. "You're trying to turn my head. You better be careful, young man, remember I'm old enough to be your mother."

"My mother is forty-two." He said

"Close," she said. My son is fifteen and my daughter is twelve, she's too young for you I'm afraid. So, have you met any local girls yet?"

He started to tell her about Elaine but decided against it. "No," he said, well I met one but she doesn't know it yet."

"You have a secret love, right?"

"You might say that, problem is she doesn't date navy guys."

"Oh, don't fall for that one," Betty said. "The right guy comes along and that will change really quick. "How do you know she don't date navy guys, did she tell you that?"

"No, she told a guy on my crew, he's been asking her out for a year or so and she keeps telling him no."

"Is she from here or Lewiston?"

"Brunswick," he told her.

"What's this girl's name?"

"I kinda don't want to say, you may know her."

"I know everybody in town, Will. I might be able to help you out or at least keep you from getting involved with the wrong kind. Come on, tell me her name." She closed her right fist and shook it at him in mock intimidation.

Will decided to throw all caution to the wind, so to speak, and confide in a person he barely knew. "Will you keep a secret if I tell you her name?"

"I promise." She said.

"Her name is Jamie, she works at the cleaners down the street," Will told her.

"Jamie Dunham," she said, "She's a beautiful girl, half the guys in town are in love with her."

Will exhaled and lowered his head as Betty smiled at his frustration. "So, it's a long line I have to get in?"

"It's a long line but I might be able to help you get to the front of the line."

"How are you going to do that?" he asked her.

"She comes in here regularly for lunch. Jamie works at

the cleaners and attends night classes at Bowdoin, the college here in town. She's always comes in on Saturdays with her dad for lunch at Eleven. You come in on Saturday and sit at the counter and I'll talk about what a nice kid you are. We'll have to take this slow, I can't introduce you to her in front of her father so I'll just arrange an opportunity for you to meet her face to face."

"That's awfully nice of you, Betty, why would you go to so much trouble for me?"

"I'm not doing it for you, I'm doing it for her. Well, actually for both of you. You're a nice boy, I knew that right away. And Jamie has had some bad luck with guys. I just think you deserve a chance with her."

"But what about her dad?" Will said.

"He lets her date anyone she wants to but a while back she fell for guy at the base and he filled her head with bullshit and then he turned out to be married."

"What a Jerk."

"Really, he was an asshole," she said, "so she has been gun-shy ever since."

e⁄ɔe⁄ɔ

Russian communication ships, posing as fishing trawlers operating in international waters, were continually patrolling the east coast of the United States, spying on US Navy ships and listening to any signal intelligence they might happen to find. The Patrol Squadrons kept a close and dogged surveillance on them, taking pictures and documenting their activities and movements. The constant presence of the Neptunes let the Russians know they were not fooling anyone and that they could not operate freely without harassment from the US Navy.

As LH-12 circled a small fleet of these trawlers, Will Cain started to understand the full magnitude of what his crew actually did. He was struck by the importance of his, and that of all the flight crew's, call to duty. Here he was at twenty years old on the very front line of the Cold War, looking down at the enemy of his country. They were doing noble work, he thought. He was fascinated by the seriousness of their job. But there were lapses in judgment from time to time. Will became involved in the lapse in judgment of his crewmate, and friend Andy Malik as the mission was ending and they were almost back to Broomstick (NAS Brunswick).

Lieutenant Powell told Will he could leave his post in the bubble and go to the rear of the plane to prepare for landing. They were crossing the coast and he wanted him to check the gear in the back and make sure nothing had come loose during the flight. Will did as he was told, stopping at the Radio Shack to say hello to Egg Money, then to the rear where Andy had already cleaned up the Unprepared meals and was sitting in one of the chairs next to the rear windows. Andy had a can of tomato soup in his hand and suddenly tossed it out the window declaring "I hate tomato soup."

"Damn, Andy, I hope that doesn't land on somebody's head." Will said.

"Shit," Andy responded. "I didn't realize we were over land. Oh well, fuck it, I can't go get it back."

Nothing more was said about it. It wasn't a big deal, Will thought, guys were always throwing stuff out of the planes when they were out at sea. They weren't supposed to but it happened anyway.

About a week later a local farmer reported to the base that a can of soup had gone through the roof of his house and ended up smashed on the living room floor. Fortunately, the family had been out of town for a few days and had only returned that day. It was fortunate for two reasons, one, no one was hurt by the object and two, the time of the event could not be determined so no blame could be assessed on which crew was guilty of the poor judgment. There were many flights in and out in that span of time.

The flak from the brass was immediate and severe. Each crew that had been in the air during those few days, when the family was away from home, was called in. Each man was questioned and advised of the seriousness of such an act, reminded that the guilty person, if found, could face charges and possibly even be kicked out of the navy with a bad discharge. No one knew anything, or at least no one admitted to knowing anything. Will told the investigators that he had been in the forward observation station as they crossed over the coast. He reasoned that, since no one was hurt by the errant can of soup, there was no good reason to ruin the life of his crewmate.

Andy Malik was terrified. He avoided Will for a while, even refusing to look at him directly but Will knew what he was thinking.

"I didn't tell them anything, Andy." He approached him and said. "I never will. I can't now anyway or they'll know I was lying before. It's behind us, just don't say anything about it to anyone, not even anyone on the crew or some girl in bed.

Andy laughed. "Thanks Will, I won't, I promise," he said, "I know I fucked up. I'll never do that again." He reached out and shook Will's hand. The matter was concluded. He had lied in a sworn statement. His dad would not be proud of him but thankfully his dad would never know.

Saturday came and Will was excited about the possibility of seeing the girl again. He spotted her as soon as he stepped through the door of the Grill. She was sitting at a table with a man about his own dad's age, who was obviously her father. She looked up and noticed him, smiled and waved at him. This caught her father's attention and he looked too but registered no emotion one way or the other. Will could see him asking her who he was. He went to the counter and sat down and Betty winked at him.

He ordered a hamburger and fries and a coke then watched in the mirror behind the counter as Betty went over to the table where the object of his affection, and the object's father, were sitting. He would have loved to know what they were saying but they were out of earshot and he couldn't hear them.

After a short while the father got up, paid their bill and left the restaurant. Will didn't know what to do so he just sat there. Then the voice of hope, inside his head, told him to turn around on the stool. He spun around slowly and saw the girl looking at him. She motioned for him to come over to her table and he pointed at himself and looked behind him, playing like he thought she might be waving to someone else. She laughed then pointed directly at him and mouthed the word 'you' and motioned again.

He did as she had ordered and she said, "sit down if you want to."

He sat down and Betty brought what was left of his meal over to him. "Don't think you can get out of tipping me by moving to another table, young man." She said.

"That hadn't crossed my mind, Betty" he told her.

"You're Sam's friend, aren't you?" she said.

Will nodded, "We're crewmates," he said.

"So, what's your name, so I don't have to say hey you?"

"Cain, William Joseph," he told her, "but I go by Will."

"So, formal," she said, smiling at him. "Well I'm Dunham, Jamie Lynn, and I go by Jamie." She held out her hand and he took it and they shook hands. So, you're a flyer?"

"More of a rider," he said. "I'm the electrician on our crew."

"Sam still comes into J & J but I was expecting to see

you with him. Where have you been?" She asked.

"Well, you told Sam that your dad didn't let you date Navy guys so I figured I'd save myself a broken heart and just never see you again."

"Oh, so you're a fatalist," she said.

"I'm not sure what that means."

"It means that you accept whatever fate comes your way. I did smile at you. I thought that was enough to at least let you know I thought you were cute."

"You think I'm cute?" he said.

"Yes, I think you're cute, do you think I'm cute? I mean you did smile back at me."

"No, I think you're beautiful," he said.

She smiled at him and looked right into his eyes. "Then why didn't you come and tell me that?"

He sighed "I don't know why. I just couldn't."

"Fear of rejection, isn't it?" she said, smiling at him.

"Yes, it's a character flaw, I suppose."

"So where do we go from here?" she asked.

"Will you go out with me?"

"If my dad says it's okay, I will. You'll have to come to the house, maybe for dinner, one night and meet my parents. Are you up for that?"

"Sure" he said, "Does your father own any guns?"

"He does but he won't shoot you," she said. "I won't let him."

Using the directions, she'd given him he drove to Dunlap Street, the street next to the cleaners, then to Federal and right. Forth house on the right. It was a nice-looking house, not rich but comfortable looking. A sign in the front yard told visitors that Richard Dunham was a CPA. And directed them, if that was their purpose for being there, to an office that appeared to Will to have been the garage at one time. A boy about ten opened the door and, upon seeing Will, shouted "Jamie, he's here." At which time Jamie and both parents came to the door. Introductions were made and hands were shaken. Then Richard directed him to come and sit in the living room while mother and daughter busied themselves with the dinner.

"Betty, the waitress at Clare's, said you are from Colorado," Richard said. "You're a long way from home but I guess that comes with a military career, doesn't it?"

Will nodded, "Yes Sir," he said, "but I'm not sure I'm going to make a career of the navy. I mean, a patrol squadron is good duty, some of the best duty in the navy but I don't know if it's what I want to do for the rest of my working life."

"Was your dad in the service?"

"A Marine, yes Sir, he was wounded at Guadalcanal and spent some time in Australia recuperating."

"Those Marines were tough boys. Did he want you to join the Marines?"

"Sort of I guess," Will said. "But he never pushed me that way. He was okay with it when I joined the Navy Reserve in high school. He didn't really want me flying all the time but I love it. Were you in the war, Mister Dunham?"

"Call me Richard, Will, we don't have to be formal. Yes, I was Airborne 101st, they dropped us in France on D-Day and we had to fight our way out of there. I've never been so scared in all my life."

"The Screaming Eagles, wow, that is impressive." Will said. "My dad's brother was in the Army. He was killed in Europe somewhere. I don't know where exactly, I never knew him. Dad said he was scared too most of the time but most Marines won't admit to being afraid."

"We all were, don't let anyone lie to you about that. It's just that when you are young you don't believe anything can ever happen to you."

"I know most of our guys feel that way because the job

we do just doesn't seem very dangerous, of course we are not at war like you were."

"Thank God for that" he said, and Will nodded in agreement. "So, Will, you know it's a father's job to look out for his kids, especially his daughter?" Will tensed up a bit.

"Yes Sir," he responded.

"Betty the waitress, she's an old friend of the family, told us a little about you."

"Really? Will replied, pretending to be surprised. "Betty is always nice to me, she reminds me of my mother a bit. I gave her a lift over to Lewiston once to pick up some things her mother had for her, met her kids and had dinner with them."

"She told us that and vouched for you, said you were quality people. Jamie wanted to invite you for dinner with us and here you are. She had a bad experience with a man from the base who led her on, talked about getting married, and then turned out to be married already. He told her he was going on Leave and would be back in two weeks but he never came back. So, you see why I am so protective of her."

"Maybe he really loved her," Will said, "maybe he got in over his head and just didn't have the guts to do the right thing. I can't imagine someone being mean like that to Jamie."

"You're too kind to him, I think, Will. He was a scoundrel in my opinion. But of course, I'm her father and it's my job to think that way."

"We're not all like that, Richard," Will said. "Saturday was only the second time I had seen Jamie but I liked her the first time I laid eyes on her. I won't hurt her, I promise you that."

"Thanks Will, I appreciate that and I appreciate your coming here to be interrogated. It's not a comfortable thing, I know. I had to go through the same thing when I first met Jamie's mother."

Dinner was congenial and the food was good. Jamie sat next to him at the table and her little brother sat across the table from Will while her mother and father sat at opposite ends of the table. The meal was nothing fancy, roast beef and potatoes, a couple of vegetables and hot rolls, but very well prepared and tasty. It was as good as he'd ever gotten at home.

The night ended with Jamie walking him to his car and inviting him back again. She kissed him before he had the nerve to kiss her first. "I'm probably going to start bringing my clothes in for cleaning," he told her, and she laughed at that.

"I want you to take me to Bailey Island on our first date." She said.

"I don't know where that is," he replied, "but I assume you do.

"I do, can we go Saturday?"

"I think so, I'll have to check my schedule. I have a flight on Friday but I think Saturday, I'm off."

"Call me when you can and let me know," she said and kissed him again.

He was still dizzy-headed when he got back to the base. He saluted the Marine at the gate when he stopped to show his ID. The Marine just smirked and waved him on. "Probably thought I was drunk," Will muttered out loud.

He barely slept that night, he couldn't stop thinking about her. It was like magic, his seeing her the first time and then with Betty arranging the second meeting. It was all too perfect. Something was bound to go wrong, he knew it was too good to be true. Still, as he looked at the note she'd given him with her phone numbers at home and at work, he could hardly contain himself. He wanted to tell everyone about her. That possibility was quickly dismissed when he thought of Sam Kinney and how he would take the news. He almost felt like he'd betrayed Sam so he knew he could not say anything to anyone in the squadron.

He wrote his mother a letter and started it with, "Mom, I met a girl." Then he went on to describe Jamie and how he'd met her. He told her about going to dinner at her house and about talking to her dad.

Ellen Cain started crying when she read his letter. She knew there was a possibility that her son might not come back home again. But just the same she wrote him back and told him she was happy for him and that he should be nice to the girl and not let her break his heart.

Egg Money, having the distinction of bunking with Will noticed the change in his crewmate before anyone else. "Did you come into some money, Will?" he asked. "You seem to be full of yourself, smiling like a fuckin' Cheshire cat. What's up?"

"Nothing, Jimmy," Will said. "I'm just glad to be alive."

"That's what I'm talking about. You shaved and put on some 'smell good' before you went out last night. Then you come in actin' happy as a pig in shit. You got laid, didn't you?"

"No, nothing like that, really. I'm just happy, I don't know why."

"Okay, Pal, whatever you say, but I smell bullshit. I know that look."

Will tried to subdue his sudden enthusiasm for life so he wouldn't have to confess to Egg Money what was really driving his zeal. He knew it was just a matter of time before everyone knew about Jamie but he wasn't looking forward to dealing with Sam.

"So, how do I get to Bailey Island?" he asked her as they pulled away from her house.

"Go like you were going back to the base and go past the base, stay on highway twenty-four all the way down. I usually have lunch with my dad on Saturdays but I begged off this morning to go with you."

"I hope he doesn't blame me for that. We could have gone later."

"It's okay," she said. "I want you to see a part of Maine that you've never seen."

"I've flown over quite a bit of it, and I went to Lewiston once with Andy Malik and Egg Money."

"Egg Money?" She said, looking at him inquisitively.

"Oh, yeah, Jimmy Watson, the radioman on my crew." He told her how Jimmy had come by the name and that Andy was another crewmate who was from Lewiston and still went home occasionally on weekends.

"Egg Money, oh—kay." She said. "What do they call you?"

"Will, usually, and some other names I can't repeat. Officially everyone goes by their last name. I mean the Officers and Chiefs call us by our last names but most of the riff raff call each other by their first names or whatever nickname that might apply."

"We are on Orr's Island now," Jamie said, "you'll be coming up on the bridge that connects Orr's Island to Bailey Island, and by the way, most people call it Bailey's Island but it's not, it's Bailey Island."

"I'll make a mental note of that." He said.

"Good, there's going to be a test later. Now this bridge," she began as they approached it, "is called The Bailey Island Bridge and…

"I think I can remember that." He said.

"Shush," she said, waving her hand at him, "this bridge is the only 'Cribstone' Bridge in the world. It's designed to allow the high tides in this area to flow through it without causing any damage to the bridge. The water we are crossing over is called Will's Gut. Turn right at the next road and then stop."

"Will's Gut?" He mouthed the words silently and rubbed his belly.

"Turn right at the next road and stop," she repeated.

He did as she told him as she continued talking. "Bailey Island was originally called Newaggin, I don't know what that means so please don't ask," he shook his head to indicate that he would not ask. "The first settler on the island was a man named William Black who was the son of a freed slave named Black Will, no relation to you." He shook his head again.

"Oh stop," she said and kept talking. "Black Will was from Kittery, Maine. William Black allegedly sold the island to a reverend named Timothy Bailey. Some say the good reverend bribed municipal officials to find a flaw in Will's title to the land and award it to him. At this point, no one really knows for sure."

"Why do they call it Will's Gut?" He asked.

"I don't know," she said.

"That's cool, Jamie, that you know so much about the state you live in."

"I love Maine, especially the coast. My folks used to bring me and my brother Carl here all the time. My dad taught me the history of the islands. Since I started working and going to Bowdoin, I don't get down here very often anymore. I didn't really have anyone I wanted to come here with until now."

"Until now?"

"Yes, you live in Colorado, we have mountains but not like you have in Colorado. Don't you just love the mountains?"

"I do, I used to spend a lot of time there growing up. I went camping and hiking a lot, but this place is as beautiful as any I've seen."

"You're just being nice," she said.

"No, I'm not, my pilot flew us up and down the coast

once for about an hour when we were coming back from a mission. I was fascinated. I've heard of the rocky coast of Maine all my life and now I'm here, thanks to you."

"Drive down this road a bit," she said, "we'll have lunch at Cooks Lobster House, my treat."

"Your treat? I can't let you pay for lunch. How would that look?"

"I invited you," she said emphatically. Besides I earn my own money. Please Will, I want to."

He consented although it made him uncomfortable but he was not going to argue with her, she was determined that she was going to pay for their meal. Egg Money didn't have any problem letting Patty pay for their dates. But he wasn't Egg Money, and it seemed strange to him, but this girl could pretty much do whatever she wanted to with him.

She ordered lobster for both of them and she showed him how to get the meat out of it. "Wrap your hand around the tail and pull it back, it will separate from the body."

He watched her do hers and then attempted to do the same but he pulled on it too hard and slung it off the table and onto the floor. She squealed with delight and laughed as he got up and retrieved it and brought it back and tried again. "Turn it on its side and push down to crack it open," she said demonstrating the technique. Finally, he managed to do as she had shown him and soon he had the meat from the tail and the two claws. "Dip it in the butter," she told him.

"This is really good." He said, with his mouth full.

"You obviously have never had lobster before."

"I've seen pictures of them but I never imagined something so ugly could taste so good."

They ate and talked for about an hour. "It goes good with beer," she said, "but I can only have a beer at home. We're not old enough to drink."

"I like beer but I'm not really a big drinker," he said, "some of the guys in the squadron, that's all they live for."

They finished eating and Jamie paid the tab. "Where to now," he asked, as they got in his car.

"Drive on down to land's end and we'll sit on the rocks of the rocky coast of Maine."

He parked the car at the end of the road and they got out and walked over to the rocks and found a comfortable spot to sit down. The waves washed against the rocks occasionally spraying them with drops of seawater.

"This is Casco Bay," she said. "We went on a boat tour out of Portland when I was a little girl. This is my favorite place in all the world. What is your favorite place, Will?"

"Anywhere you are Jamie." He said.

She looked at him for a moment. "But you don't even know me."

"I want to know you," he said.

They sat in silence for several minutes until she finally spoke. "Tell me about Colorado."

"I wasn't too forward, was I?"

"No," she said matter of factly.

"There's a place up in Coal Creek Canyon where I was hiking one winter with my dog, Boxer. A little waterfall was frozen solid and I walked out on it while water was rushing under me but the ice was thick enough to support my weight. Boxer came out on the ice too and we stood there for a half hour or so just looking up at the mountains and listening to the water rushing under our feet. It was still and quiet and I imagined it was what heaven must be like. Anyway, that following summer we went back to that spot and Boxer ran out to the waterfall and plunged into the water. I was laughing and he was trying to swim out of it. I could read his mind and I knew he was wondering why the water wouldn't support him. He got out and we went on down into the Arapaho National Forest and spent the night."

"What happened to Boxer?" She asked.

"Boxer died, he just got old and died."

"I'm sorry." She said.

"That's the problem with dogs, and cats too, if you happen to be a cat person, they don't live as long as people do, so when you get a dog, or a cat, you know you're in for hurt when they die."

"It must have been very hard to leave your home and come so far away."

"I had to move on, it was time. I always loved to fly and I wanted to fly in the navy. I didn't want to go to college and become an officer but I wanted to do pretty much what I'm doing now."

"How long will you stay at Brunswick?

"Until I get out of the Navy, at least that's what they tell me. My obligation is up in '64. I might make a career out of it but I haven't decided yet." The wind was picking up and the temperature was dropping a bit. She'd had the foresight to tell him to bring a jacket because April in Maine often brought lower temperatures later on in the day, especially on the coast.

She huddled closer to him and he put his arm around her. "I have to tell you something." He said.

"You're not married, are you?"

"No," he exclaimed, "of course not. Why would you ask me that? Oh, the guy your dad told me about. No, Jamie, I wouldn't do that, not to you or my wife if I had one."

"Okay, calm down, I'm sorry I asked," she said. "What is it you have to tell me?"

"We're going on deployment in June."

"But we just met, and you're leaving?"

"I know, they should have warned me not to meet any beautiful girls two months before a deployment. We'll be gone five months. What I want to ask you is if I can write to you and can I continue seeing you when I come back."

"Are you sure you want to keep seeing me when you come back?"

"I'm sure," he said.

"I hope so, I was so disappointed when Sam kept coming into the shop and you were not with him. I wasn't about to ask him where you were but I wanted to."

"That's funny," he said, I couldn't stop thinking about you but I'd almost given up on seeing you again. I was afraid that if I went into the cleaners it would be too obvious and might spook you. But fate played its hand and you just happened to be in Clare's Grill that Saturday." He knew it was more than fickle fate at play in their meeting but he wasn't going to tell her that, at least not now.

"So, you are a fatalist like I said."

"I guess so. I didn't know I was, but I guess I am."

"When are you leaving and where are you going?" she asked.

"We're leaving June fourth, two days after my birthday. It's a split deployment between Argentia, Newfoundland and Keflavik, Iceland. My crew is going to Iceland."

"That sounds awfully lonely, Will Cain," she said, "you'd better write me."

"I will, Jamie Dunham, every day."

"No, you won't." She said.

"I'll try to write you every day."

She had snuggled up against him as they talked and he realized their noses were almost touching. He was almost struck dumb by her face, so much so that he could hardly think straight. He thought she was the prettiest girl he'd ever seen. He cupped his left hand around her neck, pulled her closer and kissed her. The world around them went away as they sat with their heads tilted together against each other's.

"This is my favorite place too, Jamie."

CHAPTER 3

Iceland

The Dunhams had a party for will on the second of June to celebrate his twentieth birthday. He had stipulated that he was to receive no gifts, but they each gave him a pair of wooly socks to keep his feet warm in Iceland. Jamie's dad boiled some lobsters and Will demonstrated his newly learned expertise on cracking and eating the ugly crustaceans. Richard gave them each a beer to enjoy with the lobster.

"Jamie was right, the lobster does taste better with a cold beer," Will said.

"If you tell anybody I gave you beer I'll deny it," Richard said, chuckling.

"I want to thank you, Mister and Misses Dunham for the party and for everything else. My folks always made a big deal out of our birthdays, mine and my sister and brother's, it was very nice."

"You just keep safe up there in Iceland, such a God-forsaken place," June Dunham said.

"I'm going to write to Jamie while I'm gone, if that's okay."

"That's fine, Will," Richard said, "we'll look forward to seeing you when you get back.

"If you don't mind, Richard, I'd like to leave my car with Jamie. She can drive it if she wants to. I just don't want to leave it at the base for five months and I don't have anyone else I trust to leave it with."

"It's fine with me, Will, if that's what Jamie wants.

"She said she'd be glad to keep it for me. It's insured and registered so it's all legal."

"I'll make sure she takes good care of it for you, Will," Richard said.

℮◞℃◟℈

The C-130's landed and taxied to the VP-21 hangar to be loaded with the deployment cargo and all the equipment necessary to the operation of a navy Patrol squadron. By the end of day on the 3rd of June they were ready. Departure would be right after squadron muster in the morning, at which time the non-crew members of the squadron would board and begin the long boring flight to either Argentia or Keflavik.

The Iceland crews left around midnight to get a head start since their trip would be much longer. Will climbed into his nose bubble and tried to take a nap but the excitement, and the chatter on the radios prevented him from dozing off. Instead he wrote his first letter to Jamie.

If ever there was a more foreboding, desolate, more windswept barren, place than Iceland Will could not imagine it. He might as well have been on the moon for all the comfort he could expect from the coming five months of his life he would surely waste in this uninhabitable place. There were no trees, none that he could see as far as he could see. The land was covered in rocks, rocks of all sizes spreading over the horizon in all directions except seaward. This would not be the glamorous life of a navy aviator he had envisioned when he left his home to see the world. This was not the world he set out to see.

They lived in Quonset huts that had been built in WW

II. The beds were comfortable enough but the living quarters were often very hot due to the oil burning heaters that made the interior almost unbearable. Stepping out into the cold night air made many men get colds and sniffles and just served to make life even more miserable. The food was bad, not nearly as good as NAS Brunswick food which for a navy base, Will was told by those who knew, was excellent fare. At Keflavik they were served what was rumored to be powdered eggs that had been left over from the Second World War.

That which saved them from insanity turned out to be the workload. Every mission assigned to a particular crew required another crew to go through the same pre-flight preparation and readiness procedures. The backup crews were required to be ready to go at takeoff in case the primary plane went down or could not perform the mission. The first couple of months kept them going at full speed almost around the clock. The scheduling left them little time to dwell on the boredom and the lack of much of anything to do. There was a recreation building on the base where they could play pool or ping pong or cards and dominoes and such. The ground crews were on port and starboard duty which meant that they worked every day and stood ramp and hangar watches every other day. There was little opportunity to leave the base, not that anyone wanted to anyway. During their off time most of the men just sat around in the hut and played poker or wrote letters home.

Will wrote Jamie every day for the first month and then tapered off to every other day and then to twice a week. He just ran out of anything to say. Every mission was pretty much the same. The cold North Atlantic looked the same every time they went up. She answered every letter he sent her the day she received it. Her letters were much more interesting. She told him about her classes and her job and how much she missed him, and she always told him to be safe on the airplane. It always amused Will how people would say, "have a nice flight" or have a safe trip" when, once you got on an airplane, it was pretty much out of your hands.

Will had never been afraid to fly, he loved flying. It just never occurred to him that something could go wrong. They were not at war so, in his mind, that danger did not exist. But just the nature of what they did was inherently fraught with danger, whether he fretted over it or not. His only moment of fear in a Neptune came not too long after he first got on crew of LH-12. Lieutenant Powell announced over the intercom that they were going to do a "stall check". This procedure consisted of setting the aircraft controls in a predetermined climb attitude and letting it climb until it started to stall. The plane would then start to fall backwards and the nose would reverse positions, recover and correct. Everyone on the plane knew what to expect. Everyone, that is, except Will. There is, quite possibly, no more frightening thing in the world than to be on an airplane that is falling backwards out of the sky.

Will was in the bubble looking up at open sky when the airplane began to shutter and shake and come to a virtual stop in mid-air. When it started sliding backwards, Will literally yelled out loud into the intercom "Oh shit." There was laughter all over the plane from his crewmembers. "Anybody got an extra set of skivvies for Mister Cain? Egg Money chimed in. The next time they did a stall check, Will was ready for it.

Little did he know at the time that he and his crew would soon face a far more potentially dangerous incident than anything he had ever faced before. They were on a routine patrol several hundred miles out from Keflavik, listening for submarines. Andy Malik operated the sono-buoy launchers. The sono-buoys, after ejection from the aircraft, deployed upon contact with the water. An

inflatable surface float, with a radio transmitter, deployed
and rose to the surface to provide communication with the
aircraft. The hydrophones, sensors and stabilizing equipment descend below to a pre-determined depth and relays
acoustic information from its hydrophones to operators on
the aircraft. The sonobuoys were typically dropped in a
pattern, like a grid or some other array, to allow detection
of precise location by triangulation. The Trons working on
the flight deck received the information through enigmatic
sounding black boxes named Jezebel and Julie. Will never
did find out exactly what they were and how they worked.

LH-12 flew in an ever-widening circle covering thou-
sands of square miles of ocean surface. They passed to the
west of the Faroe Islands, turned south and headed toward
the British Isles. The daylight was fading and the trip had
heretofore been uneventful. Lieutenant JG Kyle Murphy,
the crew navigator mentioned that the radar was experi-
encing some glitches but did not elaborate.

Will took a last long look down at the bleak expanse of
the North Atlantic below him. From the warmth of the aircraft it did not seem threatening. But they had been trained
to both respect and fear it. They had been told that a man
could only last forty-five seconds in the water and that
meant little to most of them because no one could imagine
actually going down in the ocean. He watched the black of
night settle on the surface and he could no longer see anything past the Plexiglas bubble that kept him warm and
safe. Occasionally he'd spot a light on the surface and he
dutifully reported to the pilot but he could only speculate
on what it might be.

He was about to doze off when he heard some chatter
in his headset. Lieutenant Murphy was saying that he
smelled smoke. Lieutenant Powell told him to keep aware
and to let him know if it got worse. A couple of minutes
later Murphy, now raising his voice, shouted into the

intercom that the smell was getting stronger and then a short time later that he could see smoke drifting up from the Radome. "We've got a fire" he screamed, almost in a panic.

"Get me a heading for the nearest land," Powell responded, calmly.

Murphy was starting to panic. "We have a fire," he screamed, "we're on fire, we're on fire."

"Calm down Kyle," Powell said, "and get me a heading for land." He called to Will, "Cain, check out the Radome and see what's happening."

"Yes Sir," Will said, and he took off his headset. He crawled along the space next to the nose wheel and opened the hatch door to the Radome. The gear was ablaze and the built up pressure was released when he opened the hatch, it blew him back about a foot or so. "Shit, we're on fire." He yelled to no one in particular.

He raised the hatch that allowed access to the flight deck, stood up, and yelled loudly, "the Radome is on fire, hand me a fire extinguisher."

Sam Kinney grabbed an extinguisher and thrust it into Will's hand. "Let me know if you need any help, Will," Sam said.

The space was very confined and only one man could work comfortably but as Will crawled into the Radome with the extinguisher in his hand. Sam came down into the crawlspace and got behind him in case he had to help him get out. The spray from the fire extinguisher filled the radar equipment space and the fire quickly went out. Will continued to empty the contents all over the equipment, lest the fire start up again. When it was over, Sam took Will's legs and helped him scoot back out of the space. He had inhaled some smoke and some of the contents of the fire extinguisher and he was coughing pretty badly.

"Damn, Will," Sam said, "you saved the day. Are you

okay?"

"I'm fine, Sam, thanks for the help." He continued coughing as he crawled back to his position in the nose bubble.

"I'll tell the Skipper we're okay."

Lieutenant Powell thanked Will for his quick action and announced that they were heading for an RAF Base in Northern Ireland. Another two hours of desperate over-water flight finally brought them to Ballykelly Royal Air Force Base just outside the city of Londonderry. The sun was coming up as they touched down and taxied to the spot to which they had been directed.

Fog had settled and engulfed the entire airfield. It was so thick Will could not see even a foot past the canopy of the bubble. When they exited the airplane they had to navigate by listening to each other's voices. Will heard the distinctive accent of an Englishman advising them that the fog would lift in about a half hour and for them to just stay close to their aircraft. Lieutenant Powell told them to sit down and not try to walk around for fear of bumping into something.

Sure enough, as the British voice had informed them, the fog began to burn off and slowly the surrounding area became visible to the men of LH-12. Will noticed what appeared to be World War Two era airplanes sitting on the tarmac around them. The Englishman accompanying the voice in the fog introduced himself to the crew.

"Good morning, gentlemen," he said, "I am Flight Lieutenant Devon Merrill and it is my pleasure to welcome you to Ballykelly Royal Air Force Base. I understand you had some trouble on your way in, so happy to see you made it."

A couple of the men were talking about the emergency they had just experienced. Will had not been concerned when they were in the air but seeing the faces of his crewmates and listening to the fear in their voices, and their relief to be on solid ground, made him aware of just how serious it could have been. He learned later that it had not been the fear of ditching in the North Atlantic that caused the strife, it was the fear that the airplane would burn up before they could get down 'to' the water. The calm, professional, demeanor of the pilot, Lieutenant Powell, kept Will from panicking.

Lieutenant Powell walked over to the man. "I'm Lieutenant Arthur Powell, Aircraft Commander LH-12 VP-21. I appreciate your hospitality Lieutenant Merrill." They shook hands and Merrill said he had some transportation coming to take them to their quarters. The men would be billeted with the Non-Coms (Non Commissioned Officers).

"I see that some of your men are interested in the aircraft parked here. I'll give you a brief history if you like." Merrill said.

"By all means," Powell responded, "we'd enjoy that."

The aircraft you see here is the Avro Shackleton patrol bomber which was designed to do pretty much the same job as your P2V.

"It looks like a Lancaster Bomber," Sam Kinney said.

"Very good, Sir," Merrill responded. "The Shackleton was built on the same airframe as the Lancaster, hence the resemblance, as you so noted, Mister...

"Kinney, Sam Kinney. My dad was in the Eighth Air Force in England during the war. He taught me a lot about the airplanes that he saw when he was flying in a B-17."

"Very good, Mister Kinney, please convey my gratitude to your father for his service to my country."

Sam nodded. "I'll do that, Sir, thank you."

"So, as I was saying, the Shackleton was developed right after the war ended to patrol the seas around England and keep us safe from submarines and other threats that might approach our Island."

"What are the wood strips along the leading edge?" Will asked.

"Those wooden strips are part of the de-icing system. Alcohol is forced into the cavity behind the strips and it weeps through the cracks and melts the ice."

Shackleton patrol bomber

The non-com barracks provided all the comforts of home. The facilities made the lodging at Keflavik seem almost like sleeping under a bridge. They were assigned to separate rooms, two men to a room, with very comfortable beds. There was a bar and a gedunk (snack bar) operated by an Airman with such a strong cockney accent that no one could understand him. Will just held his money out in his open hand and told the man to take what he needed to pay for the things he ordered.

They ate in a fine dining hall and the food was what Will assumed was typical British military fare. Again, the food, like the sleeping quarters, shamed their meals at Keflavik, it was even better than what they were fed at NAS Brunswick, and the Brunswick food was generally very good.

He had tea, hot tea with real cream for the first time in his life. The US Navy ran on coffee but the Brits favored tea. Will liked it and continued to drink it that way for many years later. Sam and Egg Money got him drunk in the bar. There was no restriction on age for one to have a drink. If you were in the military, you were old enough to drink.

They worked on the damaged equipment the next day, Will and the Trons, Jimmy Beardon AT 2, Wallace (Wally) Lansky AT 3, and Egg Money. Beardon made a list of equipment they needed to replace and gave it to Sam Kinney. Will examined the electrical wiring and made a list of what he needed. Sam, being the First Mech on crew was the de facto boss of the crew and he took the lists to Lieutenant Powell, who turned in a requisition for the material.

ക്രജ

Jamie stopped at the mailbox to retrieve the mail, shuffled through it to separate the letters from Will, of which there were three. She then went into the house, left the mail for her parents on the kitchen counter and went to her room to open Will's letters. Until now she'd not received a letter from him and she was beginning to think that he was not going to write to her as he'd promised. But the first letter was dated the sixth of June, two days after their departure and she realized that delivery of mail from faraway places was going to be erratic. She opened the first letter and began to read it.

Dear, Jamie,

I'm writing this as we are crossing over the rocky coast of Maine with many hours of flight time ahead of me until we get to Keflavik. I miss you already and I haven't even left sight of the world you live in. I haven't told anyone on my crew about you yet because I don't want to stir up any trouble with Sam. Sam is a friend and I know how he feels about you. I can certainly understand why he feels that way about you because I feel the same way. I will write you again when we get to where we're going.

Will

In the other two letters he described the base and the surrounding area, how miserable a place it was to be banished to. He said they were either working or flying every day and that was what kept him from going nuts. He asked for a picture of her and told her how glad he was that he'd met her.

She showed the first letter to her mother. "Be careful, daughter," her mother said. "Will is going to be very lonely in that terrible place and he might express feelings for you that are not well thought out. He may think he is in love but, you have to admit, you two hardly know each other."

"I know, Mom, but he is different," she said. "He's not Don. Looking back, I can see now the flaws and deceit in Don that I couldn't see then because I was so infatuated with him. Will is different. He's got a good heart and a good mind. He's a good man, Mom. I know that."

"I just hope you are not falling for him too quickly."

"I miss him terribly, I don't know how I'll get through the next four months without him." Jamie said.

Her mother exhaled and sighed deeply. "My God, Jamie, you've already fallen for this boy, haven't you?"

She just pursed her lips and stared at her mother.

"But how could this happen so quickly, honey?" You saw him one time and…"

"Twice, I saw him twice," Jamie interjected.

"Excuse me, twice," her mother said. "I think you may be rebounding from Don and see more in Will than you can possibly know this early in a relationship."

"I don't know, Mother, Don never crosses my mind anymore. I just know this is right. I don't know how I know, I just know."

"Just be careful, Jamie. Use this time apart to really explore your feelings. You know one day he'll get out of the Navy and will most likely go back home."

"I know," Jamie said.

The next few months would drag by slowly as Jamie devoted herself to her job and to her classes. She drove Will's car down to Baily Island one Saturday in August and sat on the rocks at Land's End pretending that he was there with her.

⅌⅌⅌

Lieutenant Powell gave the crew the next day off. "It's not often, men, that we get an opportunity to visit a foreign country. Some of you may be of Irish descent so this will be a chance to see your ancestral home.

Sam, Will and Egg Money decided to go into town. The Brits directed them to the local bus stop where they could catch a bus into Londonderry, not too far from Ballykelly. They had a day to wait for the arrival of the requisitioned equipment before they could make repairs to the aircraft and fly out. At this point none of them really wanted to fly out. Ireland was green and beautiful and warm. They changed into the civilian clothes they carried on every flight, in expectation of the possibility that they might have to land in another country or state.

The bus driver initiated a conversation with them as soon as they boarded the bus. "You're Americans aren't you?" he said in a thick Irish Brogue.

"Guilty," Sam told him and the man laughed.

'Where are you boys from?" the man asked.

"I'm from Kentucky, originally," Sam said, "my name is Sam Kinney.

"So you're Irish?"

"That's what my dad told me." Sam replied. "This fella here is Jimmy Watson and he's from New Jersey." Sam put his left hand on Egg Money's shoulder. "And this young buck here is Will Cain from Colorado."

"Well my name is Sean Patrick and I'm from Ireland." Looking back at Egg Money, he asked, "Are you Irish as well, young man?"

"I don't know what the fuck I am," Egg Money said. The man shrugged his shoulders and Will started chuckling at his friend's honest abrasiveness. Sam just shook his head.

You'll be visiting the City of Londonderry, which is called Derry by the locals. Derry is the second largest city in Northern Ireland, after Belfast, and the fourth largest city in Ireland. The original town, The Old Walled City lies on the west bank of the River Foyle. The city now covers both banks of the river. Have fun and enjoy yourselves but be careful. Some Irish people don't like Americans because they get you confused with the English."

Will was fascinated by the town and its people. As Americans, the three of them stood out like the proverbial sore thumb but most of the people they passed or met were very friendly. Every Irishman has a relative or knows someone in America and most Irish people like Americans. There were pictures of President Kennedy in the windows of almost every shop or bar they passed.

"I'm getting hungry," Egg Money said, "let's find a place to eat.

"Me too," Will said and Sam concurred.

They came to a Chinese restaurant and Will suggested they try it. Sam allowed that it wouldn't be any good because the Irish are fond of boiled potatoes and such other bland food.

"Come on, let's try it." Will suggested again. "Chinese food is the same everywhere isn't it. Maybe they have Moo Goo Gael Pan."

"Well look at you," Sam said, "You're really starting to come out of your shell, cracking jokes and all."

"He's been like that for the last month or so," Egg Money said. "I think he got laid or something because he's been as happy as a pig in shit lately."

"Nah," Will said, "I'm just excited to see different parts of the world I've never been to before. I always wanted to travel, that's why I joined the Navy in the first place."

"You didn't go see Elaine again did you?"

"No Jimmy, I didn't. Elaine is too flaky."

"Well then you must have met a girl because that's the only thing I know that can make a man walk around smiling like a halfwit all the time."

Will brushed it off but he noticed that Sam seemed to be in deep thought about something. Will knew what Sam was thinking but he let it go.

The Chinese food was the best any of them had ever had, they all agreed. "Who would have ever thought the Chinese food in Ireland would be this good," Sam said, as he continued to eat.

At the barracks that night some of the crew went to the

Rec. Room to watch television. The Brits joined them and the Americans expressed their appreciation for the accommodations they had been provided.

Their hosts were more than happy to welcome them. One older man said, "Your fathers' generation helped save our island during the last war. We shall never forget that. Americans will always be welcome to us." Heads were nodded and glasses of Bock Beer were raised in a toast.

The British Airmen were all older men in their upper thirties and early forties. They were more or less indifferent and did not seem to share the American's enthusiasm for Ireland.

The news came on the television and film was showing riot and protests were breaking out in Belfast. It was the IRA, so said one of the Brits. "The Irish Republican Army," another elaborated further, "murderin' trash and scoundrels, if you ask me," he said.

Few of the 'Yanks' as they were called, knew what he was talking about. When some British policemen started beating the protesters with their nightsticks, the place erupted in cheers. None of the crew of LH-12 knew what to do so they neither cheered nor lamented the actions of the British cops.

The next day the replacement parts arrived and Will and the Trons spent the day replacing the fire-damaged equipment. At the end of the day, Lieutenant Powell tested the radar and announced that it was okay. "We'll be flying out in the morning, Men, get a good night's sleep." Powell said.

"Couldn't you test it a couple more days, Mister Powell?" Egg Money said, and everyone laughed, including the Lieutenant.

"Sorry, Watson, I wish I could but orders are orders." Egg Money smirked and shrugged his shoulders. "But I have a tidbit of good news," Powell added. "We'll be making a stop in Prestwick, Scotland to drop off a couple of our British counterparts. We'll get to see Scotland but we won't get off the airplane."

The fog had burned off when LH-12 lifted off the runway at Ballykelly for the short hop across the northern stretches of the Irish Sea to Prestwick. Will watched the Emerald Isle disappear beneath them then the green plains of Scotland began to appear in the distance. It didn't look any different than Ireland did from the air. They made a quick stop at the Prestwick airport to discharge their passengers and then back into the air and out across the North Atlantic toward Iceland. Will started writing a letter to Jamie.

It was back to hunting Russian submarines and surface ship reconnaissance for LH-12. The grueling routine continued and Will, and most of the crews were grateful for it because it took their minds off the drudgery of their environment. The saying was that there was a woman behind every tree in Iceland. The problem was there are no trees in Iceland, at least there were no trees in the Southern Peninsula where Keflavik was. It was a cruelly barren landscape like no place most of them had ever seen. Will often asked himself, how and why would anyone in their right mind live here? He had no answer for it.

By October it was below freezing most nights and early mornings. Pre-flight preparation was a miserable ordeal, rain would stick to a man's face and freeze, causing the eyes to tear up and then the tears would freeze. Thankfully they had pre-heating equipment for the engines so the delay before takeoff was shortened substantially.

Just before the approaching date for departure of the squadron, around the end of October, an incident occurred that Will had been dreading ever since his first date with Jamie Dunham. The squadron mail clerk, an efficient and extroverted Airman named Bernie Gordon delivered the mail to the LH-12 crew's Quonset hut. Since the hut was unoccupied, because the aircraft was overdue for arrival from a mission, Bernie left the mail on each man's bunk.

When Will came to his bunk he noticed a stack of letters lying on the cover. Something seemed amiss, there were two letters, one from his mother and another from his sister. The two letters were lying together and three other letters, all from Jamie were turned sideways across the other two. They looked as if someone had picked them up and then just tossed them back on the bed rather than laying them down neatly on the stack. He looked around but saw that no one was watching him. But Sam was standing by his bunk checking his own mail, or pretending to be checking his mail. That's how it appeared to Will. "Crap," he said out loud. He should have told Sam right away, that would have been the better thing to do.

Sam walked by Will's bunk on his way to the showers and said nothing. He didn't even look at Will.

He saw the letters, Will was convinced now. He wasn't sure what to do. It really wasn't like he'd busted up a romance between Sam and a girl. Sam had never gotten more from Jamie than how much he owed for his cleaning. It wasn't like he was sleeping with Sam's wife or girlfriend. Sam would have to be reasonable and accept this. It just made no sense to inject strife into their friendship and working relationship.

He went over to the base rec. building to read Jamie's letters. She had gotten his letter about going to Ireland.

"I'm so jealous," she wrote. "My last name is English and I've always wanted to go to the UK. In another letter: "I drove your car down to Land's End where we sat on the rocks and kissed right before you left for Iceland. I've been studying and planning on what we'll do when you come back and sitting here missing you. Luv ya! J."

He put the letters back in their envelopes and stuffed

them down in his seabag. He didn't write any more letters because he would be back in Maine before they would have time to get there.

Sam remained outwardly and noticeably aloof to Will, barely looking at him and only speaking to him when it involved the crew or the aircraft. It was an awkward situation. Sam Kinney was not just a friend, he was, as First Mech, the boss of the crew. Will did not imagine Sam would hold that against him. Sam was too professional for that. But Will didn't really know how to handle the friction between them so he just kept quiet and waited to see what would happen.

CHAPTER 4

Winter of '61

It was snowing when the squadron landed at NAS Brunswick. Nevertheless, a crowd of people awaited their return. Wives and kids and others were allowed to gather in the hangar to avoid the snow. LH-12 taxied to the ramp and was directed to its position. The crews would have two days off to get resettled into the barracks. Those going on leave would settle in, stow their gear and head out as quickly as they could pick up their papers.

Fleet Air Wing 3 had provided some temporary butane heaters to keep the hangar a little more comfortable for the dependents and friends who had come to welcome their men back. Hot coffee and donuts were made available. This was a happy time for the men of VP-21, coming home. Coming home was so much better than leaving home, especially for the married men.

"Gonna be some bottom knocking tonight," Jimmy Watson said, to anyone in earshot, as the men began to exit the aircraft. They tied down and secured the plane and gathered their gear for the walk to the barracks. Some would get rides from friends. Will would call Jamie from the barracks and see when she could bring him his car. He was looking forward to seeing her after five months of being away. She had written that her folks were planning a welcome home party for him.

"Your girl is here waiting for you, Will," Sam Kinney told him, without smiling but also without any evidence of angst.

"Where?" Will asked, looking around at the crowd gathered in the hangar.

"I saw her from the cockpit, standing in the hangar."

He picked up his seabag and suitcase and started walking toward the hangar. He spotted her waving her arms to attract his attention. She was wearing a sock hat with a ball on top, a heavy coat, denim jeans and snow boots. Her blond hair protruded from underneath the sock hat and framed her face. "She's beautiful," he thought. His smile turned into a grin as he approached her. He sat his gear down and ran to her. She wrapped her arms around him and kissed him like she never had before. "Welcome home, Sailor," she said in his ear.

"You didn't tell me you were going to be here," he said, kissing her again.

"I hope you don't mind."

"Heck no I don't mind, He said, "I love it, thank you Jamie, and I love the hat."

"I have to change clothes before I go off base and I can't take you in the barracks with me so you'll have to wait outside a few minutes."

"I've been waiting five months, a few more minutes won't hurt me."

He took his belongings into the barracks, found his assigned sleeping quarters and changed clothes. Ben Wattigney had remembered that Will liked living on the second floor so he put him in with Egg Money again. It was just as if they had not been gone for five months.

The Dunhams were preparing dinner for him and seemed to be genuinely glad to see him. Jamie took him into the living room so they could talk. "Tell me about Ireland," she said.

He did tell her, going into elaborate detail of every minute he'd spent there. He told her about Londonderry and
the Chinese restaurant and the RAF base. "It's a beautiful
place," he said, "but there's a lot of strife between the au-
thorities and the citizens. I don't really understand the pol-
itics of it but I'm not sure why the British are even there."

"Did you meet any girls?"

"No," he said and kept right on talking.

She drew back, furrowed her brow and expressed mock
outrage. "No. just no? That's all you have to say. I must
say, Will Cain, you are frustrating sometimes."

"What did you expect me to say?"

"I was hoping maybe for, No, I didn't meet any girls,
why would I meet any girls when I have you?"

"Oh, well then I must say, Jamie Lynn, I did not meet
any girls in Ireland, why would I meet any girls when I
have you?"

"Okay that's better," she said.

Their relationship was a strange affair, he thought to
himself. She acted as if they had known each other for
years but they had not. They had not been intimate yet,
except in his dreams, but it did not bother him. He knew
he had fallen for her and she acted as if their love for each
other was an established fact. He wondered if perhaps this
lovely girl he wanted and needed so badly was just flighty
and in love with the notion of being in love. Was she using
him to get over the guy who did her wrong? He had to
consider that possibility and that she might fall out of in-
fatuation with him as quickly as she had apparently fallen
into it. He also had to examine his own feelings about her.
Was it her looks, she was a beautiful girl, or did he go after
her just to prove to his friends and the world that he could
get a beautiful girl like her? He didn't honestly know, and
he grew dizzy just thinking about it.

He took her hand in his and caressed it with his other

hand. "Jamie, I guess you've probably figured out by now that I'm in love with you."

"You are?" She said. "Oh Will I was hoping so, I wanted to tell you how I feel in a letter but I just wasn't sure you felt the same way. I love you too."

"I'm not sure how you could not know how I feel about you," he said. "I mean I get all goofy when I'm around you and I can't take my eyes off you. Come on, you had to know."

"I didn't," she told him. "I'm not as self-confident as I sometimes seem to be. I'm a bit forward, I know, but I think it's just an act to hide my fear of betrayal. I mean you could get out of the navy tomorrow and leave here and never see me again."

"No, I don't get out until February of '64, that's over two years from now."

"But how many more deployments between now and then?"

"I don't know," he said, "but it doesn't matter. Nothing is going to change with me. Oh, by the way, Sam knows about us."

"Oh my gosh." her mouth was wide open and she covered it with her hand. "How?"

"Our squadron mailman left your letters on my bunk in Iceland and Sam apparently noticed the pink envelopes and looked at them. He hasn't said much to me since then."

"I'm sorry, Will, but believe me I never gave Sam any indication that I had any interest in him."

"I know you didn't, Egg Money—Jimmy Watson, keeps telling him that but I guess Sam is just hooked on you and can't get passed it. He'll have to now."

At dinner, Richard Dunham asked Will about his trip to Northern Ireland. Will told him about the Brits cheering the police on when they were beating the protesters and said he didn't understand what that was all about.

"Northern Ireland is a separate country from Ireland. It is made up of predominantly Irish Protestants, who are British loyalists, and Irish Catholics. The Protestants are a majority of the population and therefore rule the country. Most of them want the British there. They are like our "Tories" during the Revolutionary War, they remained loyal to the British."

"So what would happen if the British leave?"

"The fear amongst the Protestants is that the Catholics would persecute them and make life miserable for them. The whole Irish thing is a real tragedy."

"Well it's a beautiful country," Will said, I'd like to go back someday."

"I hope you do, if that's what you want," Richard said, but I doubt the British Soldiers who are stationed there share your enamor for the place."

"One of the British Non-Coms said they all liked Americans because our father's generation helped save their country in the war. I wanted to tell him about you being in the Paratroopers and dropping into France on D-Day but I couldn't because my friend, and crewmate, the guy who has a thing for Jamie, was in the room. I just wasn't ready to let him know about Jamie and me at that time. He knows now and I don't know how that's going to work out."

"Well, Jamie tells me it was all in his mind so I expect he'll come to accept that, and hopefully it won't affect your friendship with him."

"I hope not," Will said.

"How about Iceland?" Jamie asked him. "You ever want to go back there, Will?"

"No," he responded. "I don't even want to think about that place ever again."

"You may recall, Will, that I told you it was a God-forsaken place," June Dunham said.

"I do, and you were right, how did you know? Have you

ever been there?"

"Oh, no, I've heard stories, that's all. I hope you never have to go back."

</sub>

Examinations for rate promotions were coming up in January and Will started studying for his E-5 rate. E-5 designated the pay-grade and AE-2 designates the Rating for which he would be testing. Jamie's logic was that they would study together at her house. Will wasn't sure if he would be able to concentrate but to his surprise she turned out to be serious about making her grades and she left him pretty much alone while he hit the books acquiring the necessary knowledge level and learning the responsibilities of the position to which he aspired. He'd passed every navy test he had taken so far and his confidence was high that he would advance to E5. It would mean more pay and that more would be expected of him.

Lieutenant Powell informed him that a commendation would be placed in his permanent file for his work in fighting the fire aboard LH-12 prior to their landing in Ireland. Sam Kinney also received the same commendation. It seemed a bit silly to Will because he only did what any man on the crew would have done had they been in his place. He just happened to be in the right place at the right time.

He asked Jamie to go to Portland with him to shop for gifts for his family and for hers. He had not as yet been to the state's largest city and he did not know his way around. A lot of the guys from his squadron regularly went drinking in Portland but he never had. "You don't have to get me anything," Jamie told him as they were on the road to Portland.

"Oh, okay," he replied, "that will save me some money

to spend on other people." He sneaked a look at her and smiled, then laughed at the shocked look on her face. "Oh come on, you knew I was joking."

She smiled sheepishly and said, "It really would be okay, if you don't have the money, for you not to get me something."

"No it wouldn't," he said, "and you know it wouldn't. Even if it were okay with you it wouldn't be okay with me. You know I'm going to get you something, you're my girl. I brought you something back from Ireland."

"You did?" She exclaimed loudly. "What did you bring me, let me see it."

He turned the car into a parking lot and parked. Pulling a small jewelry box out of his pocket he opened it up and removed a Shamrock emerald necklace.

"Oh, Will," she said, "it's beautiful I love it but you shouldn't have done it. It looks expensive." She was crying now and he assured her that it did not break his budget."

"Turn around," he told her and she complied. He put it around her neck and clasped it in the back.

"How much did this cost you?

"I'm not going to tell you," he said. "I wanted you to have it. It looks beautiful on you." The truth was he'd spent his monthly flight pay and a two-week paycheck on the necklace. Before he met Jamie he never imagined he would ever spend that much money on a girl. But he did it and the tears in her eyes made him glad he had. Sometimes you just have to go a little crazy to keep from going insane.

"I don't know what to say, Will, no one has ever done anything like this for me, thank you."

"That's okay," he said, I wanted to do it. I'll just skip a couple of car payments and…

"Oh you—you, oh I don't know what you are." She slapped him on his chest with her hand. She kissed him and then kissed him again.

"Hold on, you're going to get us arrested. Save your kisses for later."

"I can't wait to show it to my mother, she already thinks you are too good to me."

I don't think I am," he said. "I'll have to come shopping again alone to get your gifts for Christmas but I need you to help me pick out stuff for my mom and dad, for your mom and dad, for Carl, and for my brother and sister. We have our work cut out for us."

"No problem, I love shopping."

"I was afraid of that," he said.

While most of America pretty much shuts down the week of Christmas, Russian Submarines do not, and for that reason the search for them does not stop. Christmas was on a Monday and the Dunhams invited Will to spend the day with them. As it turned out he had a flight on Saturday and would be off on Monday so he looked forward to spending Christmas day with them. He'd sent the gifts home to his family and the things he'd bought for the Dunhams were under their tree along with all the others. They were treating him like family and he enjoyed the feeling.

Would it ever come to that?" he didn't know. He could imagine it happening but so many things could go wrong. He didn't really know Jamie Dunham and she didn't really know him. For that matter he didn't really know himself. Would he wake up one morning and not have the same feelings for her? God, he hoped not but how many twenty-year-old men know what they might do tomorrow. He loved her, he knew that for certain, but what would life with her be like. She got on his nerves on occasion but every girl he ever knew got on his nerves after a while. He needed something real in his life and Jamie was the real thing, he believed. Elaine Meador showed him that something could be great but not real.

He fell asleep on the Dunhams' couch after Christmas dinner and was awakened by Jamie in late afternoon. She wanted to go for a ride. "Let's go watch the ice skaters in the park." She said.

Will pulled the car into a parking space on Maine Street at the park in front of the First Parish Church where a pond froze over in the winter and the town kids came to skate. "I used to come here and skate when I was a kid. Can you ice skate, Will?"

"I've tried it," he said, "but I'm not very good at it."

"We'll have to go to the rink at Bowdoin sometime. I love to ice skate."

"Whatever you say, Jamie."

"Oh, you're still sleepy, aren't you? I'm sorry I woke you up."

She slid over next to him and laid her head on his shoulder. "Can I ask you a question?"

"Sure," he said.

Without looking up at him she said, "Why have you never tried to get in my pants?"

"Wow, I was not expecting that," he said. "I don't know for sure why, I guess I was just afraid."

"Afraid of what? She said.

"I don't know that either, afraid of messing things up if I came on too strong, I guess."

"You want to, don't you?"

"Yeah—I do, if you knew how much it would probably scare you. I never met anyone like you, Jamie. I never had a girl I was afraid of losing. I just don't want to lose you."

"I want you to make love to me, Will," she said, still not looking at him.

"Okay," he said."

"Well that went well, I was hoping you wouldn't put up a fight."

"But where will we go? I can't take you to my place. I

mean the guys wouldn't mind but it would be a distraction." She laughed at that. "I'm not going to do it in the car. I love you and I don't want it to be just a cheap thrill."

"The family of a good friend of mine, Sarah Miller, has a cabin on the river. She'll give me the key if I ask her. We used to go there on some weekends with other friends, no boys, when we were in high school."

She said she would set it up for the following weekend. He took her home and drove back to the base to get some sleep. LH-12 was due a maintenance check and he'd be working all day Tuesday.

"You look like a man in love," Jimmy Watson said, as they were getting dressed for work.

"I am, Jimmy, I truly am. I guess it shows, huh?"

"Damn right it shows. There's only two things can make a man walk around like he's in a stupor the way you've been walking around for the past few months, love and dope. And I know you ain't takin' dope. So I was right about you and the Cleaners girl wasn't I?"

"Yep," Will said. "I fell for her that day we went in with Sam to get his clothes. I tried to hide it but that didn't work. I'm just sorry for Sam, I know he liked her."

"Yeah, I know," Jimmy said. "Sam has been acting very moody lately. I don't know if it has anything to do with the girl or not, but he seems out of sorts to me."

"I hope he isn't mad about it. You know. I'd like to say that if he'd been going with her I never would have pursued her but I don't know if that's true or not." I fell for her right away.

Jimmy nodded, "I know you did, but as for Sam, it was all in his head. Don't worry about. He'll get over it."

"I hope so," Will said.

Will had finished replacing the number two DC generator and was cleaning the engine de-icing brush blocks when the Commanding Officer, Commander C. E.

Mackey approached him, along with Lieutenant Powell. Will stood up and saluted them. The Commander and Lieutenant Powell returned his salute. "Cain," Commander Mackey said. I have just approved your commendation from Lieutenant Powell for the job you did fighting the fire on your aircraft when you were airborne on this last deployment. I wanted to congratulate you personally on a job well done. You may very well have saved your aircraft and the lives of everyone on board."

"Thank you, Sir," Will said. "Anyone on board would have done the same thing."

"Just the same, you are the one who did it so congratulations and thank you."

"Yes Sir," he repeated, "thank you." Lieutenant Powell winked at him and nodded his head.

It was hard sometimes to take the navy seriously. It often seemed as if they were just playing war like he did when he was a kid. The commendation looked good on a resume' but it really was total bullshit. He had put out a fire on the airplane that 'he' was riding on. That didn't seem like an act that would warrant a commendation but he wasn't going to tell the Commanding Officer that.

Saturday came and Will was up early at a time when most of the men who didn't have duty were still asleep. As far as Jamie's parents knew, he and Jamie were spending the day together, going skating and having lunch and such stuff. He shuddered to think that her folks would find out what their real plans were. But he quickly put it out of his mind. Jamie was watching for him from their front window and she came out right away and got into his car. She slid over against him and lay her head on his shoulder which had become a common practice for her lately. He put his right arm around her and pulled her closer to him.

"Where to?" he asked.

"Go to Maine Street and right. At the bridge turn right

on Route One. Are you still up for this?"

"Not yet," he said, "but I will be soon."

"What? No, that's not what I meant, silly, I mean do you still want to?"

"Why would you ask me that?" he said, surprised at what she had said. "Did you think I'd change my mind?"

"I was just teasing you."

"Don't scare me like that."

She giggled and kissed him on the cheek. "In about three miles you'll be turning left. I'll let you know when."

He turned left as she directed and drove a couple of miles farther where she told him to turn in. It was a quaint log cabin, not very big but very rustic looking, sitting in a clearing right on the Androscoggin River.

After turning on the furnace, she took his hand and led him into the bedroom and turned to face him. They just stared at each other for a few moments. "Nothing will ever be the same again for us, Jamie." He said.

"I don't want it to be the same Will, I want it to be better, and it will—Will."

"You're stuttering again."

ౡ

In January testing was done for rate/Rating promotions. Three months later the results were received and posted. John Dolinski made Chief Petty Officer (CPO), Andy Malik was promoted to AD1 and Will made E-5, AE2, Aviation Electrician's Mate 2nd class. Many others on the other crews also were promoted. Many failed to pass their tests and were passed over. Jimmy Watson allowed that "it would take a war for some of these dickheads to get promoted."

It was announced that Chief Ray Purcell would retire after twenty years in the Navy. His service began

December 10th 1941, just three days after Pearl Harbor.
Like so many of that generation, Ray Purcell had answered
the call in his country's time of need. Will liked to think
that he had joined the Navy 'for the cause' but it wasn't
the same danger and hard times that were faced by the men
of Ray Purcell's era. Now as he was being 'Piped' out of
the service, on his way back to Alabama for whatever life
that might be waiting for him, The Commanding Officer
ordered a hand salute. Every man in the squadron, including the officers, gave the Chief his only official salute.
John Dolinski became the Chief of the Electric Shop.

Will and Jamie had dinner at Clare's Grill. His friend
Betty was off because she worked the day shift. They were
holding hands across the table. It was a fitting end to a day
at Sarah's cabin. "Here's to Sarah," Will said, raising his
water glass up for her to clink.

"To Sarah," she replied and their glasses clinked together.

"Maybe we should buy that cabin."

She just smiled at him.

"Jamie," he said.

Yes, Will."

"Will you marry me?"

"Yes I will—Will." She giggled when she said that.

"Why don't you just call me William if Will—Will is
just too funny to pass up?"

"I can't help it, I'm sorry." She said. "I'd love to marry
you, but where will we live?"

"We can get a place near the base, or an apartment in
town. I'm going to formally ask your dad for permission."

"That's a little old fashioned, don't you think?"

"Yes, it is, but it's respectful and I'm an old-fashioned
kind of guy."

"That's sweet, Will, I like that. Yes, you ask my dad
and I'll pretend we haven't already decided yet."

"What if he says no?"

"Then I'll marry you anyway. He'll forgive me, I'm his only daughter."

Walking out of the café onto the sidewalk, Will spotted Sam Kinney staggering toward them. "Oh shit," he said quietly to Jamie. "Sam Kinney is coming our way. He looks like he's drunk."

Sam was indeed drunk. Jimmy Watson told Will that Sam had been drinking heavily ever since Iceland. Sam approached them with a look of anger on his face. "What's up Sam? Will asked him, trying to defray any confrontation.

"I'm shitfaced, Will and I'm pissed off."

"What are you mad at, Sam?" He moved Jamie behind him with his arm and stood between her and Sam.

"You got her, Boy, you knew how I felt about the bitch and you just went on and got her." Sam was fuming and slurring his words.

"Come on Sam," Will said. "We're friends, don't do this.

"Fuck you, Will Cain, I ain't nobody's friend, and fuck her too. You probably have been ain't you?" Sam yelled, attracting the attention of some people passing by. They looked back but walked on.

"Calm down Sam, I'm not going to let you talk to her like that."

"I'm going to tell that bitch what I think of her, and I'm just drunk enough to do it." He tried to walk around Will and reached for Jamie.

Will hit him in the jaw and Sam went to the sidewalk, still cursing. He managed to get up and started walking to his car which was parked on the street in front of the café.

"You're too drunk to drive, Sam," Will said. Let me take Jamie home and I'll come back and get you and take you to the base."

"Fuck that," he said, "I'm going to Lewiston and you can't stop me."

"I wish you wouldn't, Sam. You're too drunk." But Sam was already in his car. Will watched as he pulled away from the curb and banged into the car parked in front of him.

"Hopefully the cops will get him before he kills himself or someone else."

"What would I have done if you had not been here?" Jamie said.

"I don't know, maybe he wouldn't have been that way if I had not been here. Damn, Jamie," he said, "If you had rejected me I would have slashed my wrists but I wouldn't have tried to get any of the blood on you. I'd have gone off to some secluded spot where I could die alone and in peace."

"You're a sick man, Will Cain. I guess that's why I love you."

Sam did not show up for muster the following Monday morning. Lieutenant Powell called the crew together. "Anyone have any idea where Sam is?" he asked them. "It's not like him to not show up for work. Watson, Cain, you guys see him lately?"

"I saw him Saturday night, Skipper, he was drunk, very drunk," Will said.

"Nobody else said anything. "Did he say anything to you, Cain?"

"Not much, Sir, he said he was going to Lewiston and I tried to talk him out of it because he was so drunk. He told me to fuck off."

"Okay," Powell said, "he'll turn up, I guess. I can cover for him for a day but if anyone hears from him be sure to tell him to get his ass back to the base."

Will was worried now. He hadn't told the boss every-thing that had happened and he was afraid something might have happened to Sam. It didn't take long for his fears to be realized.

Word came the next morning to the squadron that witnesses had seen a black and yellow Chevrolet plunge into the Androscoggin River about 2:00 a.m. Sunday morning. Police were conducting a search for a body but heretofore none had been found.

Wednesday night, when Will knew Jamie would be in class he went to her house to talk to her father. June Dunham answered the door. "Jamie is at school tonight, Will, she won't be home until nine."

"I know, Mrs. Dunham, I came to talk to you and Mister Dunham." She showed him to the living room where they both had been having coffee.

"Would you like a cup of coffee, Will? June asked him.

"No ma'am," he said, "thank you anyway."

"What's on your mind, Will?" Richard Dunham said.

I wanted to maybe get your advice on some things, if you don't mind." Richard motioned for him to continue.

Well, when I get out of the Service in February of '64, and I still haven't decided if I want to make a career of the Navy yet. I mean I like what I'm doing but there's no guarantee that I will be able to stay in VP-21 or even at Brunswick. Anyway, I'm an Aircraft Electrician and I could probably go to work for a commercial airline in Portland. Also, I don't remember if I told you this or not but my dad has a chain of hardware stores in Denver and Colorado Springs, well not a chain but four in Denver and one in Boulder."

"That qualifies as a chain, Will," Richard said.

"Oh, right," he continued, and my dad has always wanted me to come and learn how to run a store and eventually how to run the whole business. I'm not sure if I really want to do that but it would be a great opportunity for me, if that's what I decide to do. But I really like it here in

Maine."

Both June and Richard were smiling now as Will rambled on and on.

"Will, does this conversation have anything to do with Jamie?" Richard asked him.

"Oh well, yes, Richard, it does. I'm not sure how to say this so I guess I'll just say it. I love Jamie, I really do. What I mean is I'm in love with her." I want to marry her but I don't want to take her away from Maine unless you think it's best for both of us. I can stay in Maine or go home and take over my dad's business when he retires."

"Well you are a man with some potentially positive options. I think you're a fine young man and I'd be proud to have you for my son-in-law but as for marrying my daughter that is strictly up to her. It's her decision. Go ahead and ask her, I wish you the best."

"He said it's up to you if you want to marry me or not." Will told Jamie.

"Let me think about it," she said and waved the key to the cabin back and forth in front of him.

"Don't your friend's parents ever get suspicious when you go by to get the key?"

"Nah, Sarah had an extra key made for me a month or so ago. I just call her to make sure no one is going to be there when we go. But summer is coming up and the Millers spend a lot of time at the cabin in the summer."

"That's not the only bad news," he told her. My crew is going on deployment in May and June to Puerto Rico."

"Oh no," she said, "why didn't you tell me?"

"I just did, I didn't know until yesterday, it's just two months. I'll write you every day."

"I'll be there when you climb down out of your airplane."

Bad news came about Sam. The police found his body several miles downriver. His ID was in his pocket so there was no need to go any further in identifying the body. They shipped him back to his folks in Kentucky.

CHAPTER 5

Roosevelt Roads

In 1919 the future U. S. President, Franklin D. Roosevelt, then Assistant Secretary of the Navy, toured Puerto Rico, visiting Ceiba. When he returned to Washington he expressed a liking for the terrain where the base is now located. This was in the World War I era and Roosevelt believed the United States could benefit from having an airfield in the location. While Puerto Rico is a Commonwealth, its territorial rights belong to the United States, which made it perfectly feasible and ideal for the American government to build an airplane base in Ceiba.

It took many years for the United States Government to become convinced of the need for an air base in Ceiba. When Adolph Hitler and Nazi-led Germany began to invade other European countries, The US, led by then President Roosevelt, entertained the idea of a Naval Air Station in Ceiba. With war in the European and Pacific theatres they began to see the necessity of the airbase. The base was inaugurated but scaled down to maintenance status with a public works office in 1944. From then until 1957, the base went through many shifts, being opened seven times and closed eight times. Meanwhile it remained as a source of employment for the citizens of Ceiba and the surrounding area. In 1957, it was upgraded to naval station status.

In May of 1961, elements of VP-21 flew into Roosevelt Roads to begin ASW and surface ship surveillance operations in the Atlantic Ocean and the Caribbean Sea. The first thing Will Cain noticed was the size of the base, it was huge, 8,700 acres in all. They were quartered in wooden barracks that looked like they had been built during the war, they were comfortable, nevertheless.

LH-12 had a new First Mech after the death of Sam Kinney. Andy Malik, now an AD1 moved to the cockpit to take over Sam's responsibilities. The pain of Sam's death permeated the mood of the crew of LH-12. Sam had always been a top-notch First Mech who was highly respected by the pilots and the crewmen as well. No one on the crew, except for Will and Jimmy Watson, knew any details of what had actually happened to Sam. Jimmy knew that Sam had been drinking heavily but Will had not told him of the events of the night Sam was killed and he had no intention of doing so. Jamie saw it in the newspaper and wanted to blame herself until Will convinced her not to fall into that trap. Sam's death was a self-inflicted wound, Will told her. He had an unprovoked and unrequited love for a woman he could not have and was unable to accept the realities of life.

Andy turned out to be a good First Mech. He had tested for E-6 the last time around because Sam convinced him that he would be a good First Mech., if not on LH-12 then perhaps on another crew and that would be a good career move. He was almost ashamed that he was happy to be riding in the cockpit now. It took the death of a friend and crewmate for it to happen and he took no pleasure from that fact.

While preparing for a flight, Will felt Andy looking at him intently, inquisitively, and he knew what he was thinking. "What can of soup, Andy?" Will said.

Andy smiled and nodded. "You're a good friend, Will,

that can of soup would have ruined me in the navy."

"I told you not to ever mention it again." Will said. "You are not in my debt. If we forget about it and never let it come up in conversation, then it never happened. It never happened, Andy, I don't know what you're even talking about."

Andy nodded and never mentioned it again.

Will wrote a letter to Jamie and one to his mother.

> *Dear Jamie,*
>
> *We arrived at NAS Rosey Roads safely, flew through the Bermuda Triangle and did not disappear. That would have really annoyed me. This is a beautiful place. We are surrounded by mountains. There is one mountain that gets rain every day. You can't see the top because it's always misty.*
>
> *I'm flying regular missions just like in Brunswick but it's a lot warmer here. Check that, it's hotter than hell here. Fortunately, we'll only be here a couple of months. I'd like to maybe get married in August when I get back if that works for you. I am going to write my mother and tell her about us. My folks are going to love you. Trust me on this.*
>
> *I love you, Will*
>
> *Dear Mom and Dad,*
>
> *I am in Puerto Rico at the Roosevelt Roads Naval Air Station. It's beautiful but hot. I will*

be going back to Brunswick in August.

    *Do you remember the girl, named Jamie,
I mentioned a few times in my letters? Well,
turns out she 'is' the one. We are getting married when I get back, maybe in August or September. Tell Dad that Jamie's father was in
the 101ˢᵗ Airborne in the war. He dropped
into Normandy on D-Day. Her folks are good
people, they already treat me like family. I'll
call you when I get back to the world.*

    Love, Will

After a month of port and starboard duty, Lieutenant
Powell told the First Mech to call for muster of the crewmembers and tell them that they have the weekend off.

"Listen up guys," Andy said," Daddy has given us the
weekend off and he says we can borrow the car. We're
going to Montego Bay, Jamaica guys." He said. "Mister
Powell is going to drive us there.

"What's in Jamaica?" Jimmy asked.

"Jamaicans," someone said.

"They got any white women in Jamaica?"

"One," Andy said, "but she has a boyfriend."

"Dammit, just my luck, why can't we go to Bermuda?

"Too expensive, Egg Money, Jamaica is a poor man's
paradise."

The airport in Jamaica was right on the water and the
approach was across a long expanse of shallow, green water through which Will could see rocks and other for-
mations on the bottom. Once they secured the airplane
they caught cabs to the Holiday Inn, at Lieutenant Powell's
suggestion. It wasn't cheap but it was reasonable. Immediately they all headed out to get a beer and to check out

the opportunities.

There were bars on every corner and bars in between. The Trons, except for Egg Money, went with the Officers and the rest of them, Will, Jimmy, Andy, and the new man on crew, Andy's replacement at Second Mech, Larry Dawson and the AO (ordinance man) Gerald Lowery, went along together.

Andy Malik drank in moderation, as did Jimmy Watson. Both had been friends with Sam Kinney and his death had made both of them consider the consequences of getting so drunk you were out of control. "I'm First Mech now," Andy said. "What if the Russians declared war and we had to fly out tonight? I wouldn't be much good to my crew if I was shitfaced."

"That's good thinking, Andy," Egg Money said. "I'm glad to see you are starting to grow up."

"Me, what about you?"

"I'm settling down, I think it's time I got married and had some kids."

"Bullshit," Andy said. "You gonna marry the egg lady and raise chickens?"

"Nope," Jimmy said. "I'm going to find me a real girl, in fact, I see one now. Look over there." He pointed across the room at a table full of girls.

They all looked and, sure enough, there were four girls who, according to Jimmy, were not ugly.

"Go talk them up, Andy and bring them over." Jimmy said.

"No, Egg, you go," Andy replied.

"You're better looking than me," Jimmy countered. "Except for Will, you got the best-looking girl in the squadron. Lowery dates pigs and Dawson is a fruit."

"No, I'm not," Larry Dawson said. "Fuck it I'll go talk to them." He stood up, downed the rest of his beer, and walked over to the table where the girls were.

"Well kiss my ass," Andy said, as he watched Dawson coming back with the four girls in tow. "He must have showed them his dick. They don't call him mule-dick for nothing."

Introductions were made and the group started pairing up. The one generally considered to be the best looking, a girl named Paula sat down by Dawson and he quickly put his arm around her. "This is Andy," he said and in turn, introduced Will, Jimmy and Gerald Lowery. Two girls, Stephanie and Gloria, sat down beside Will, Rose picked Andy.

Egg Money reprimanded them. "He's off limits, Girls," as Will raised his hand.

"I'm taken," he said.

"Oh, but he's so cute," the one named Stephanie said. "Why can't I have him?"

"I'm sorry, Stephanie, I'm flattered but my heart belongs to a girl back home."

"I don't want your heart, Gorgeous," she said, "I'm after your body."

"That belongs to her too." Will told her.

She frowned and said, "what a waste."

Jimmy grabbed her hand and pulled her into his lap, the other one, Gloria, sat down by Lowery.

Andy ordered two pitchers of beer and all previous thoughts of 'growing up' or 'getting married and having kids' were forgotten for the time being.

Will awoke early the next morning, Jimmy and Stephanie were in the next bed. The door between the two adjoining rooms had been left open and the two double beds in that room contained, respectively, Andy and Rose and Larry Dawson and Paula.

They slept for hours, all eight of them had gotten 'toes up' drunk, as the saying went. From what Will could tell, since it was dark in the room and judging by the noises that had prevented him from sleeping most of the night, the couples were not too drunk to consummate their newly established, albeit temporary, relationships.

At around eleven in the morning, Andy awoke and wanted to go to breakfast. It took an hour for everyone to get showered and dressed but eventually they left the rooms and headed to the hotel dining room.

Lieutenant Powell called the room and Will answered the phone. "Cain, we're flying out at eight o'clock in the morning. Don't let the guys get shitfaced tonight," he said.

"I'll do my best, Skipper," Will said, "but they don't listen to me very much."

"Well, just appeal to their common sense and dedication to duty."

Will laughed at that.

"Yeah, I know," Powell said, just do your best, Will."

The girls, as it turned out, worked as secretaries at a Brokerage House in Miami. They were leaving early Sunday morning as well so they all settled for dinner out Saturday night with no heavy drinking and only a quick roll in the hay but no spending the night.

Will kiddingly chastised Jimmy for jumping into bed so quickly with the girl from Miami. "I thought you loved Patty the egg lady," he said.

"I do," Jimmy replied, "but when love goes up against horny, horny wins every time."

After the flight back on Sunday, they were back at work on Monday prepping the plane for a late-night mission.

On deployment, the workload was much harder, especially when the squadron was split up. Fewer planes had to do the work that was usually done by twice their number. This put a heavier burden on the flight crews and on the ground crews as well. This was not necessarily a bad thing because it made the time go by faster and kept their minds off personal business. When they were not flying, the flight crews worked in their perspective shops to help maintain the aircraft. It was hot in Puerto Rico and the work was sometimes very demanding.

Changing parts on the back of the engines required a man to straddle the landing gear doors in order to reach the work area. For a man of Will's height, he was 5' 11," it was not as difficult as for a shorter man. Sometimes the legs would give out and Will had seen a man fall out of the wheel well on several occasions, especially when it was as hot as it was at Rosey Roads.

As thorough as their safety training was, there were some things that no one ever told you. No one ever cautioned Will about vacating the nose observation station on landing approach. The pilot or the First Mech usually told the man in the bubble to leave the space before they began approach. The one time this did not happen, Will began crawling back along the corridor to go to the back of the plane. When he was about halfway to the flight deck hatch, the nose gear came down and he was looking out at blue water a thousand feet or so below him. Had the plane made a sudden sharp turn to the right he would have ended up in the ocean below. One learns by experience and he never did that again.

Another time he saw a man almost tossed out of the rear window of the plane when the pilot made a quick turn to the left to check out something he'd seen on the surface. The men would often raise the window covers and snap them in the open position, especially in warm weather. On this occasion, they were flying low and slow circling a trawler and taking pictures. Prop spray was hitting the man in the port side seat. He was raised up to better look out at the activity below when the plane turned sharply and he had to grab the sides of the window to keep from falling out. He sat back down and closed the window covering, shaken a bit but not seriously traumatized.

They often threw trash out at the Russians but rarely did anything ever actually hit the target. Will enjoyed the rocket runs. He had the best seat in the house sitting in the bubble watching the water come up to meet them and then looking up at clear blue sky as the plane climbed out of the run. It was exciting and exhilarating.

Will turned twenty-one on 2 June while they were in Puerto Rico. The guys took him drinking in Ceiba and they shot some pool in a local pool hall. Larry Dawson had just come on crew to replace Andy Malik at Second Mech, when Andy was advanced to the cockpit. Dawson had a reputation for having a quick temper, as well as his already established boldness with women. This character trait, or, more appropriately, it might be called a flaw, got them into some hot water in a Ceiba pool hall.

Typically, when a man scratched, sank a ball in the wrong hole, he had to spot a ball. Well, the owner of the pool hall didn't want them spotting a ball because it delayed the game and he charged them by the game. Dawson spotted a ball and the man took it off the table and put it back in the pocket. Whereupon, Dawson removed the ball and put it back on the table. The man repeated his action, yelling at Larry in Spanish. He struck the man with his pool stick and knocked him to the floor.

Several customers came rushing in to take up for the owner, who happened to be related to many of his customers. A fight ensued and the lot of them were yelling and punching and tossing the Puerto Ricans around like rag dolls. They vacated the premises and found another place to celebrate Will's birthday.

When he returned to the barracks, Will found a birthday card from Jamie. "Happy twenty-first, Stud, I love you," was all it said.

CHAPTER 6

Autumn Leaves

LH-12 and the other two crews that had accompanied them on the Rosey Roads deployment arrived in Brunswick on the first of July. There was not the huge crowd that had greeted them on their return from Iceland since only three planes were returning. Jamie was there to meet Will just as she said she would be. They immediately drove down to Bailey Island and sat on the rocks at Land's end.

"I missed you," he told her. "I don't do guy stuff anymore and it's awkward for the crew. They think I'm turning into a wimp."

"Are you growing tired of me and longing for the good old days?"

"No, Jamie, that's not what I meant. I'm telling you that because it's funny. "I'm kind of out of place on the crew now and that's okay. I'm able to see now how stupid it is to act the way most of the guys in the Navy act. They go drinking and chasing women and I sit on my bunk and think about you. I wouldn't have it any other way."

"Tell me the truth, Will," she said. "You're not getting cold feet, are you?"

"No, I'm not, Jamie, but I am starting to reevaluate whether or not I want to stay in the Navy. I thought that was what I wanted but now all I see is a one deployment

after another to this or that shithole when I'd rather stay
here in Maine. We've got another five-month deployment
coming up in January."

"Oh no, where to this time?"

"Sicily," he said, in January."

"Oh God, so far away. What will I do without you for
so long?"

"The same thing I'll do, I hope, sit around and miss me
the way I miss you."

"Do you still want to marry me?" she asked him.

"Of course, I do," he said. But here's what I want to do.
Why don't we get married now, by a JP? And then we can
have a formal wedding when I get back. That way we can
go ahead and file for benefits and military insurance, in
case I 'buy the farm' on deployment."

"Does 'buy the farm' mean what I think it means?"

"Yes, but don't worry about me. I'll be okay"

"Please don't say such things, not even in fun."

I'm sorry," he said, but if you dwell on the worst things
that can happen it just keeps you upset all the time."

"I'm just afraid you'll forget me while you're so far
away," she said.

"Don't get silly, I've never liked silly girls. I fell in love
with you in the cleaners that time, the first time I ever met
you. Nothing is going to change, baby, I won't change,
ever," he assured her.

"No, I don't expect you will" she said. "Okay, whatever
you think is best, Will. I'll have my teaching degree by the
time you're out of the Navy so I can work after we're married."

"Good, I'll just go fishing every day, or play golf."

"You don't want me working, after we're married?
That's what I've been going to school for. I want to work
Will."

"I don't mind, Jamie, I really don't. I just want to take

care of you—us and the kids."

"Oh, so you want kids right away?"

"I'd like that. Don't you think our kids will be beautiful? I'm good looking and you are the prettiest girl I've ever seen, so how can we fail?"

"I'll make your babies for you, Will Cain. It'll be my pleasure."

You'll probably be cursing me when they come out. My dad said my mother cursed him like a sailor when I was born, something about my big head."

"You're teasing me, Will. I will never curse you for anything. You've made me happier than I've ever been in my life. After the first time we met, I was happy just anticipating when I'd see you again."

"Oh yeah? well I was miserable worrying that we never would."

"It was a miracle, I knew it would happen," she said.

"It was sort of a contrived miracle, Jamie. I plotted to make it happen."

"And how did you do that?" She asked him.

He told her the whole story about how Betty had helped him meet her.

"Oh, gosh," she said. "That is great, I love that you'd do that just to meet me. I'm going to have to go thank Betty for the conspiracy."

They were married in July and Will found a place near the base, a trailer house which was about all he could afford at the time. Richard Dunham sat down with the two of them in his living room and offered an alternative plan.

I know that when you first get married you want to be on your own, and I know that you, Will, want to take care of your wife and anything that comes along later—kids, I mean. But just from an economic and logistics basis I'm going to suggest that you live here with us for the time being.

Will was uncomfortable with the plan at first but Richard made the case that, since they only had one car that Will needed to get back and forth to the base, it made sense for them to live with the Dunhams so Jamie could more easily get to work and to school. Richard and June had their bedroom downstairs so Jamie and Will would reside upstairs and have the run of the house. The only negative was that Jamie's brother Carl also slept upstairs but they could live with that. When Will was back from Sicily they could then decide where they wanted to live and whether or not Will wanted to make a career of the navy. He relented and agreed that living with Jamie's parents was more logical than the course he would have chosen.

Will insisted they pay rent to the Dunhams and help with the utilities and such. Jamie received fifty dollars a month from the Navy for dependent benefits and both parties agreed that amount would suffice for their share of the living expenses. He ultimately had to admit that living with the Dunhams was like living with his family at home and he got to sleep with their daughter. It was a pleasant home life for the both of them.. Having her alongside him in the bed, was a good way to spend one's life.

July turned to August and then September. Will and Jamie spent every available minute together. When he was not flying and she was not either working or going to school, they were either at Bailey Island or in Portland or Lewiston. It was at the Rollodrome in Lewiston that Will's brief time in Maine came back to haunt him. He and Jamie were skating. She was much better at it than he was but he was holding his own.

They sat down at a table to drink a coke and her back was to the door. Will saw Elaine Meador walking in the door with Bobbie Reynolds and Andy Malik's girlfriend, Jeanne Randall. "Oh shit," he said to himself, but Jamie heard him.

"What's wrong, Will?" she said.

"Nothing, well maybe nothing. A girl I knew before I met you just walked in. She hasn't seen me yet."

Jamie turned around to see who the girl was. "Who is she Will?"

"Don't look, I don't want to attract her attention. She's a little crazy."

"Oh, come on, how crazy can she be? Call her over here, we can compare notes on you."

Ah, crap," he said, "here she comes."

Elaine had spotted Will and was headed toward his table. He waited for the confrontation he knew was coming.

"So, this is what you threw me over for, you asshole?"

Jamie recoiled and gave her the kind of look usually reserved for streetwalkers and drug addicts.

Elaine persisted, "you quit me for this skinny bitch."

"She's not skinny, Elaine," he yelled then realized how stupid that sounded. Jamie gave him a look of disbelief and placed both her hands on her hips.

"But I am a bitch?"

"No, Jamie, that's not what I meant," he said. "I don't know why I said that. I didn't know what to say. What do you want, Elaine?"

"I just wanted to see what the bitch looks like. She looks pretty damned skinny to me." Jamie turned to face Elaine defiantly.

"Don't look at me like that, Bitch, "this asshole got what he wanted from me and never called me again. Now I see why."

"Yeah," Jamie yelled at her, "I see why too. You're trailer trash."

"Listen you," Elaine said. "I was screwing' him before he ever met you."

"Well you're not screwing him now EeLoon," she said, butchering Elaine's name insultingly, because I am."

"Both of you please calm down," Will said. "Elaine, Jamie is my wife. I'm sorry I hurt your feelings but I knew her before I met you," he kind of lied to her.

"You married her?" Elaine yelled, and for a moment Will thought she was going to cry but she didn't. Instead she yelled at him, "fuck you, Will, and fuck her too," and she stormed off and left the skating rink, with her entourage in tow, leaving Will relieved that only words were thrown and no punches.

Jamie was laughing as they got into the car and Will started laughing too after he got out of the parking lot. She was full of herself. "That's the first time I've ever stood up to anyone like that. I'm glad you don't think I'm skinny."

"I'm sorry about that, Jamie, I really am. I just sort of panicked. I was afraid she would try to hit you and I didn't want to have to hit a girl but I would have if it had been necessary."

"Look at the bright side," she said. "That's twice we've both been told to eff-off together. Sam said it that time outside Clare's and EeLoon just said it again. So, we're a team."

"Looks like," Will said.

"So, answer me this. Did she have to beg you to go to bed with her like I did, or did you jump in right away?"

He looked sheepishly at her but said nothing.

"You jerk, you went down easy, didn't you? Why Will? that hurts my feelings.

"Because she's not the girl I've been dreaming about all my life. She's not the woman I want to make my babies for me. She's not the woman I cannot live without. She's not, Jamie, no one is, you are.

She started crying and slid over beside him and laid her head on his shoulder.

∽∾∽

In October, the Defense Department learned that Nikita Khrushchev had begun a plan to place Soviet nuclear missiles in Cuba as a counter to the possibility of another attempted invasion of the island. The United States had installed nuclear missiles, aimed at Moscow, in Italy and Turkey. Khrushchev and Fidel Castro had signed a secret agreement in July of '62 and construction of several missile sites had begun in late summer.

In mid-October, the Air Force Sent a U2 spy plane to scan the suspected areas and it was confirmed that Soviet Missiles were being installed in Cuba. Negotiations began and President Kennedy demanded that the missiles be removed and the launch sites deconstructed. On October 22, the President went on television to notify the American people of the presence of the missiles and explain his decision to order a naval blockade around Cuba. He also made it clear that the U.S. was prepared to use military force to remove the threat to national security if Soviet refusal made it necessary.

Several VP Squadrons were immediately deployed to Guantanamo to assist in the implementation of the blockade. VP-21 would not join the deployment but would send four crews to supplement the squadrons under full deployment. The VP-21 crews were to be: Lh-3, LH-5, LH-8, and LH-12, Will's crew.

He called his folks to tell them and he told Jamie and her family. The news was not happily received. But orders were orders and strangely somehow Will was excited to go. The night before their departure Will went home to the Dunham house. When he found Jamie, in their room, he could tell she had been crying.

"I want you to knock me up, Will. If something happens to you I want a part of you to keep on living."

"Nothing is going to happen to me, Jamie, I promise. It's just routine. Don't get me wrong I'm not trying to talk you out of anything, but don't worry about me."

She laughed through her tears. "I intend to worry about you, that's my job."

"Where are your parents and Carl?"

"They're visiting some friends in Portland," she said: "They won't be home till around midnight. I think they vacated the house for us for our last night together until you come back." He gave her that look and she knew what he was thinking. She took his hand and started kissing him as she reached for the switch and turned off the light."

CHAPTER 7

Guantanamo Bay

The U.S. Naval Station at Guantanamo Bay, Cuba is on the front lines for regional security in the Caribbean area. The base supports the ability of U.S. Navy and Coast Guard ships, along with allied nation ships to operate in the Caribbean area by providing contingency and quality logistical support with superior services and facilities.

The U.S. first seized Guantanamo Bay and established a naval base there in 1898 during the Spanish-American War. In 1903, the U.S. and Cuba signed a lease granting the United States permission to use the land as a coaling and naval station. The U.S. and Cuba signed a treaty in 1934, granting the U.S. perpetual lease. Both the U.S. and Cuba must agree on any termination of the base.

In October of 1962, LH-12 and the other three aircraft from VP-21 flew into Leeward Point, Guantanamo Bay to begin operations in the southern Caribbean to assist in the naval blockade of Cuba ordered by President Kennedy.

The patrol Squadrons were housed at Leeward Point, to the west across the bay from the main base which is called Windward or Seward. Seward is much like a small American town with housing sub-divisions, for married personnel and their dependents, baseball fields, and restaurants.

Several thousand American dependents had already been evacuated and taken back to the United States until the perceived danger to them was ended.

The runway at Leeward was so close to the Cuban land border that aircraft on approach from the west were required to make a sharp right turn in order to line up for landing. Not too many days before a Boeing 707, loaded with ammunition had crashed while landing at Leeward killing the seven-man crew and creating a thunderous explosion that some thought looked like a mushroom cloud.

The VP-21 crews and support personnel were quartered across from the Marine Barracks. Jimmy Watson found a bunk and saved the one next to him for Will. They had bunked together ever since Will had joined the squadron.

"What am I," Will said, "a security blanket for you? Somebody is going to think we are married or something."

"Nope, I just like you and I'm a creature of habit. I just feel more comfortable with you close by."

Will, smiled at him, "I do too Jimmy, thanks for saving me a bunk."

Sam was the only friend I had except for you, Will," Jimmy told him. Nobody calls me Egg Money much anymore."

"You want me to start calling you Egg Money?" Will asked him.

"Nah, it's not really the same with Sam gone."

"Then why did you mention it?"

'I don't know," Jimmy said.

The next morning, Will was awakened to strange noises coming in from outside the open window near his bunk. It sounded like dogs or some other animals growling and snarling.

"That's the Marines," Larry Dawson said. "I was here on deployment about a year ago with VP-11 and I found out from one of the Marines that they sit out close to the fence and fuck with the Cubans on the other side, growling and yelling shit at them. But they're out there to keep the Cubans from coming across the fence and, in case of a shooting war, to give us enough time to get to our planes and haul ass. So, don't nobody say any shit about the Marines."

"My dad was a Marine, Larry," Will said. "I have no problem with the Marines."

Soviet ships approaching the quarantine zone were stopping at the 500-mile line and lying dead in the water. LH-12 came upon a Russian submarine in an area east of the Bahamas. They notified the Navy and two American Destroyers showed up and began to escort the Sub out of the area.

Will had spotted the ship when it was several miles away and alerted Lieutenant Powell. As they approached Will got on the intercom again. "That looks like a sub, Skipper." He said.

"It's a Sub alright," Powell replied. "Good work, Cain."

Wow, this is fun stuff, Will thought. He had begun to really appreciate the importance of his job. They were flying almost every day and half the airplanes were in the air at any given time for the first week they were there.

On the 28th of October the Soviet leader, Nikita Khrushchev, agreed to remove the Russian missiles from Cuba in exchange for a promise from the United States to respect Cuba's territorial sovereignty. The actions resulted in Fidel Castro's accusing the Russians of backing down to the United States and relations between Russia and Cuba worsened.

Two years later Khrushchev was removed from power by Soviet hard-liners who were angered at his withdrawal of the weapons. The crisis was effectively over but the VP-21 contingent would remain in Cuba through November.

The food at Leeward was even worse than the gruel

they had been served at Keflavik. Will never thought that was possible but it was a fact. They had been told that the food on the other side was the best anywhere in the military. The whole crew was given a day off and they went as a group to see how the other half lived. The nine enlisted men on the crew boarded the ferry for the ride over to Seward.

Andy Malik the First Mech, Larry Dawson, Second Mech, Will Cain, the Electrician, Jimmy Watson, Radioman, Gerald Lowery, Ordinance man, Jimmy Beardon, Lead Aviation Electronics Mate (Tron), and Wally Lansky, Junior Tron were enjoying their first day off since arriving at Guantanamo Bay.

They found the chow halls to be as had been described to them. The food was excellent and the amenities were top notch. They went to a movie and bought ice cream at the Gedunk.

"This is almost like being at home," one of them said, "except there are no women."

"The dependents have all been evacuated," Andy Malik informed them. "And if they were here you couldn't hit on them because every one of them is either someone's wife or daughter."

"That sucks," Jimmy said and they all agreed.

That afternoon they caught the ferry back to Leeward. They had a mission in the morning and morning came early at Leeward.

Back at the barracks, Will was standing at his locker sorting out miscellaneous articles of clothing while Jimmy was getting ready to go take a shower. Jimmy left the Cube and headed toward the Head, a short while later he returned and sat down on his bunk.

"I thought you were going to take a shower," Will said.

"I was, but Dawson is in there."

Will looked bewildered. "And?" he said.

"I don't want my pecker to get an inferiority complex." Jimmy replied.

"Are you serious?"

"Yes," he said.

"But why?

"Come on, I'll show you."

"You're kidding me, right?"

"No, come on," Jimmy insisted, and he took Will's arm and pulled him toward the Head.

"I don't need to see it," he protested, to no avail, because Jimmy kept pulling him along with him

He took him over to the shower area and yelled, hey Dawson, turn around!"

Larry Dawson turned around to see who was calling him and Will saw the object of their conversation.

"Holy shit," he exclaimed, "you weren't kidding." He immediately turned and went back to his bunk, laughing all the way.

"You're not normal, Watson, there is something wrong with you," Dawson said.

"Well if you're normal, Larry, nobody else is." Jimmy said.

He found Will in their Cube, still laughing. "What's so funny?" he asked.

"I can't believe I just walked into the Head to check out another man's dick."

"Well if you get out of line I'll tell Jamie about it."

"She won't believe you," Will said.

"I'll take Dawson as a witness."

"That won't be necessary, Jimmy," Will said, "I won't get out of line.

Their last mission in Cuba took them out over the Windward Passage between Cuba and Hispaniola. The hop had been uneventful until about three hours in. Will spotted an object on the surface, at about nine o'clock, too far away to make out even with the glasses. He alerted the cockpit and the plane turned in that direction. As they approached it became clear that it was a small ship or boat of yet unknown origin or purpose.

It turned out to be a Cuban Navy gunboat and seemed to be headed no place in particular. Lieutenant Powell told Lowery and Dawson to man the cameras in the aft station of the plane. He began to circle in preparation for a run on the boat. They started the jets. It was procedure to start the jet engines when flying under 400 feet. The plane dropped down to about a hundred feet off the water and about fifty yards from the ship. They made several runs, low and slow, around the ships as the cameras took pictures of the little boat.

"Smile, assholes, you're on candid camera," Will said to himself.

The ship's Gunners manned the deck guns and were tracking LH-12 as it circled them several times. From the bubble, Will was looking right down the barrels of the Cuban guns. For a brief moment, Will had a terrible thought that, were they to be shot down and he were to die, he would have lied to Jamie about not getting killed in Cuba. That seemed to be his only concern, not the dying but the lying. It would not have been an actual lie, of course, he reasoned, since his dying in Cuba, or the avoidance of same, was not something anyone could have predicted with any reasonable expectation of accuracy.

It appeared that everyone on the ship, including the cooks and below deck personnel had come topside to see the show. Will remembered their briefings before every flight in which they were told that, were the Cubans to actually fire on them, a team of Marine Crusaders (Vought F-8) was always not too far away, perhaps just over the horizon, just waiting for such an event and would respond quickly and blow the ship out of the water. It was little comfort to the Neptune crews except for the fact that the Cubans knew about the marines as well. They were not going to shoot LH-12 down, Will assured himself.

The pilot announced that they would make a couple more passes and then continue their mission. Will watched the guns still following him, as if they were aiming at him and him alone. The ship's crew could easily see him and it seemed they were trying to spook him. He waved at them and they waved back. He extended his middle finger at them and to his surprise and delight they returned the favor.

A sudden impulse came over him. Not wanting to be outdone, he took off his flight suit, pulled down his dungaree pants and skivvies and shoved his bare bottom up against the Plexiglas canopy that surrounded him, in full view of every Cuban on the ship. They all started laughing and pointing at the airplane. Will regretted that he would never be able to see the pictures of the laughing Cubans he'd mooned.

❧❧❧

Back in Brunswick Jamie was anxious for Will's return. They would have the month of December together before he left again for Sicily, and then she would wait five months. Her mother tried as best she could to comfort her daughter.

"It'll be over before you know it, dear. You're young and everything seems more urgent when you're young. He'll only be gone five months. You can devote yourself to your education and prepare for the rest of your life."

"I know Mother, but it just seems that, now that I've found the man I want to be with for the rest of my life, the navy keeps ruining it for me. They don't need him as much as I do."

"Jamie," June said, "I know that you and Will want to be together, but he had this job when you met him and you knew that the service always is an erratic life-style. Just be thankful we are not in a war. That would be an even more terrible thing for you to have to contend with."

"I know Mother, I just want everything to be perfect, and it will be one day, I know that."

"I know that you two were sleeping together for some time now and I'm really glad you got married but don't try and make him do something he doesn't want to do."

"Like what, Mother?"

"Like insisting he get out of the navy and settle in to a boring, dead-end job he doesn't like. Have you ever watched his face when he talks about those damned air-planes? Taking him away from something he loves could cripple his spirit. Let him make that decision."

"I will," she said, "and we weren't sleeping together, Mother."

"Oh, come on, Jamie, I'm your mother, I know that look and the way you two acted around each other. You're telling me you hadn't been to bed with Will before you were married?"

"Oh, we made love ten or twelve times, but we never went to sleep."

"You're teasing me, daughter. It's not nice to tease your mother like that," she smiled at Jamie.

"I couldn't resist. Will is everything I've ever wanted and needed in a man. I love him, Mother, I love him so much I can't stand it. It was not wrong because I knew we would get married sooner or later. I'm just happy that it was sooner."

"What if he decides not to stay in the navy and go back home to Colorado when he gets out?"

"I'll go with him if he wants me to and if he stays in the navy I'll wait for him to fly back in just like I've been doing."

"Trust me, Jamie, he'll want you to. I've never seen a man so lovesick as Will is. He may not have told you but he came and talked to us while you were in class one night. He told your father that he'd stay in Maine if we wanted him to."

"He's told me that too, and I'd like that but I'd also like to go home with him," Jamie replied. "I think he'd be happier back home in Colorado."

"It's a choice the two of you have to make. Your father and I have already accepted him as our son-in-law so you have our blessing. We couldn't be happier that you've found the man you wanted to marry."

"Thank you, Mother," Jamie said. "That means a lot to both of us.

Jamie was waiting at the VP-21 hangar when LH-12 arrived. She ran to him and threw her arms around his neck, wrapped her legs around his waist, and kissed him long and passionately. After he changed clothes they drove to 'home' for dinner. "Jamie is spoiling me," he told the Dunhams. "Not many guys have someone waiting for them when they come in off deployment, especially someone who looks like Jamie. She was a big hit at the squadron. There were five guys talking to her when I got off the plane."

"They were nice, Will. They kept asking me if I needed anything, water, coffee or coke or something. They all knew you and kept telling me what a great guy you are. One of them said that, if I ever decide to dump you, I should look him up. I told him that was not going to happen."

"That was very considerate of them," Will said, "I mean to be so concerned about your comfort and all."

"Well, I thought it was very nice."

"How was Cuba, Will? Richard asked him.

"Hot," Will said, "very hot, and when I get back here it's forty-seven degrees. It felt like the dead of winter."

He told them about the base at Guantanamo Bay, how it was laid out, with the patrol squadrons at Leeward, and how they rode the ferry over to the other side, and about the missions they flew. He told them about the food and the fence and the marines but he did not tell them about mooning the Cuban Navy ship. He'd tell Jamie another time. He wanted to share that with her alone. He also never told anyone about Jimmy Watson dragging him into the shower to verify that Their Second Mech, Larry Dawson, was an extremely endowed man indeed. That was not something he'd likely put in his memoirs.

They still went to the cabin every weekend in December just because they had become so fond of the place and because it was a little awkward at the Dunhams, with Jamie's mom and dad downstairs and Carl just down the hall. Their love was such that they could hardly keep their hands off each other when they were together. Their proper behavior in the presence of Jamie's parents fooled no one, but the parents kept their silence. "We were like that too when we first got married Richard Dunham told his wife. What's the worst thing that can happen?"

"She could get pregnant," June said crossing her fingers to indicate that she hoped it would happen.

"Then we'll have a grandkid. I expect we'll have a whole house full of grandkids one day."

Christmas of '62 was both joyous and sad. Will was happy to have become an integral part of the Dunham family but Jamie was almost traumatized over his coming departure. They made one last trip to Land's End and sat on the rocks. He again pledged to her his undying and unwavering love for her.

"You are the very best of every person I've ever known," he told her. 'I don't love you just because you're beautiful—that helps—helps a lot." She smiled at his sincerity. "And not because you're great in the sack, and you are great in the sack."

"You are too," she interjected.

"Don't stop me, I'm on a roll. I love 'you', Jamie because I love 'me' when I'm with you. You make me proud of myself. I could never live without you, not ever."

But life goes on, as the adage goes, the good and the not so good, and on the fifth of January 1963, VP-21 departed NAS Brunswick for NAF (Naval Air Facility) Sigonella, Sicily.

CHAPTER 8

Sicily

The squadron had a new Commanding Officer for the Sigonella deployment. Commander C.R. Robertson, USN, took command in November of 1962 and would serve in that capacity until October of 1963.

The first stop on the trip to Sicily was Lajes Airbase in the Azores Island. The base was home to elements of the Portuguese Air Force as well as a detachment of the US Air Force. It was at Lajes that the men of VP-21 discovered how much better the American Air Force personnel lived than the men of the US Navy. They were provided with rooms instead of open Cubes and the food was superior even to that which was served at Brunswick.

The lush green islands were beautiful and the people were congenial. It amazed Will that these tiny dots of land out in the vast expanse of ocean could be home to people who must surely feel isolated from the world. He wondered how they got here and what made them decide to stay here and create a society.

At the base store, Will bought some things to send home to Jamie and her parents. There were many books about and other items indigenous to the islands. Will listened to a brief history of the Azores, by the manager of the store, just to 'expand his horizons', so to speak.

"There are nine major Azorean islands in an islet cluster, in three main groups. These are Flores and Corvo, to the west, Graciosa, Terceira, Sao Jorge, Pico and Faial in the center, and Sao Miguel, Santa Maria, and the Formigas Reef to the east. They extend for more than 370 miles and lie in a northwest-southeast direction."

"The vast extent of the islands defines an immense area of 420,000 square miles. The westernmost point of this area is 2,100 miles from the North American Continent. All the islands have volcanic origins, although some, such as Santa Maria, have no recorded activity since the islands were settled. Mount Pico, on the island of Pico is the highest point in Portugal, at 7,713 ft. The Azores are actually the some of the highest mountains on the planet, measured from their base on the surface of the Atlantic. Because these once uninhabited and remote islands were settled over a span of two centuries, their culture, dialect, and traditions are widely varied.

The man knew his history of the islands and had no doubt delivered the same soliloquy hundreds, or at least dozens of times before. The effort paid off and the flying sailors spent a lot of money on souvenirs and such. Will bought Jamie a picture of Ponta Delgada, the Capital city of the islands, and made arrangements to mail it to her before he left.

Ponta Delgada

Ponta Delgada is on the island of Sao Miguel and Lajes is on Terceira so he would never see the city in the picture he bought for Jamie. He just bought it on a whim.

The next leg of their journey took them to Naval Station Rota, Rota Spain for two days of rest, of which only the pilots got very much. They say that travel is educational and Will was convinced it was so. He had been many places since joining the Navy. He was, in his opinion, becoming quite urbane and cosmopolitan. His love for the life he was living, was growing with each new place he visited and with each new assignment. Now he was headed for Sicily, something he could only have dreamed about a few years ago. He wondered to himself if he'd be able to give up this life easily for a more mundane existence. But his mind would just as quickly take him back to the life waiting for him back in Maine.

He pondered these things as they flew by Gibraltar on their way to Sigonella.

Two Neptunes of VP-21 pass Gibraltar 1963

The U.S. Naval Air Facility at Sigonella, Sicily (It was not called a Naval Air Station in 1963) actually consisted of two bases. The main facility, where the barracks, chow hall, and base offices and support facilities were located was referred to as Naf 1, and the airfield, about nine miles south, which consisted of a hangar and a small chow hall for those working there and for the crews, was called Naf 2.

Construction of the airfield was completed in August of 1959 just three and a half years before VP-21 arrived in 1963. The aircraft were parked on remote concrete pads, with sufficient distance between them to make it difficult for an attacking aircraft to take out more than one plane with one bomb or rocket.

The area is prone to flooding from frequent heavy rains and the men of VP-21 discovered that almost every time it rained the power went out. They also learned that the power system was 50 cycles instead of 60 cycles like in the U.S. They had to purchase small converters in order to use their electric shavers or radios.

The drive between the two bases was interesting to one with any sense and appreciation of history, as Will had. Huge trees lined both sides of the road and their limbs covered the road. This had served to permit the movement of troops and material along the road without their being spotted from the air. At one point in the road, as you rounded a curve, two concrete bunkers had been built on either side of the road. "German machine gun emplacements," their duty driver explained to them. "No telling how many Americans came upon this place unknowingly and were shot all to hell before they could back up and get out of the way."

"Fucking Krauts," Andy Malik commented. "I hope they all died here.

"Ask Weber," Jimmy said, "his dad was probably stationed here. He knows all about shit like this."

Erik Weber was a German citizen whose family had remained in West Germany after the war was over. He had joined the Navy in anticipation of earning his US citizenship. Weber worked in Power Plants and was said to be a very good mechanic. Some of the men didn't trust him but Will found him to be congenial enough and he figured everyone should have a fair shot at becoming a citizen if they really wanted to. Most of the people he knew took their American citizenship for granted but Erik Weber, having been born during the war and in the war understood the value that he and the other men of VP-21 had not earned but rather had received by default. For Weber, and men like him, their service in the navy was how they earned that privilege.

Also, along the route there was a farmhouse, about a hundred yards off the road, with one end of the house caved into a pile of rubble. It was said to have been blown down by American tanks in the battle for Sicily, because Germans had fired on the approaching troops from inside the house. Now, almost twenty years later it had still not been repaired.

NAF Sigonella sits at the foot of Mount Etna, one of

the most active volcanoes in the world. Etna is in an almost constant state of activity and smoke can be seen billowing up out of the crater on clear days. It was an impressive sight, even for a boy from Colorado who grew up in the Rockies and was accustomed to seeing snow-capped peaks. Colorado has a number of high peaks over 14,000 feet above sea level, Pike's Peak and Mount Elbert being the most prominent ones, but Etna is 10,991 feet above sea level and it sits on a base that is at sea level. Pikes Peak sits on a base that is 6,000 feet above sea level so the peak itself is about 8,000 feet. Etna is higher than the Rockies, technically speaking.

Mount Etna Sicily

Will vowed that he'd go up the mountain before he left Sicily. He would accomplish that in April when the navy provided a bus to take men on a daytrip up to the high ground for all who had similar ambitions.

In the meantime, they were flying missions with ever increasing frequency. The Mediterranean was teeming with ship traffic, on the surface and below it and they dropped their sonobuoys and listened for Russian subs, snapped their pictures of anything and everything they found. They flew around in great circles looking for the bad guys. In March, they flew over Palermo and, much to the surprise and delight of the crew of LH-12 they got to see The Big E, The USS Enterprise CVN 65, docked in Palermo. Lieutenant Powell made several passes so everyone on the plane could get a look at the pride of the fleet. Will was ecstatic. He could never have imagined the thrill of the job he was allowed to do. It was everything he ever wanted to do. Riding in this wonderful airplane and flying over the most famous aircraft carrier in the navy. He was awestruck for days after. He'd had the presence of mind to bring a camera with him on every mission and he snapped several pictures of the Enterprise. He sent some of the pictures home to his folks and the others to Jamie.

Andy and Jimmy decided they wanted to check out Catania and Will went with them. It was an old city, older than any city in the United States, with a strange mixture of new and old. Centuries-old churches and government buildings contrasted with supermarkets, Shell gas stations, restaurants and coffee shops. The Americans were instantly recognizable and approached by one local after another. Some wanted cigarettes and others wanted money. It seemed that every human being in Sicily, including the kids, ten and eleven-year old boys, smoked cigarettes, but apparently, few bought them. They preferred American cigarettes.

They could buy cigarettes in the Ship's Store for fifteen cents a pack, or a buck-fifty a carton with a limit of two cartons a month. Will didn't smoke so he used his allotment to buy cartons for his fellow crewmembers who did smoke. Dawson and Lowery smoked and Jimmy Beardon, one of the Trons, also smoked. Non-smokers were very popular if they were willing to furnish their friends with cigarettes.

A couple of base personnel saved up their monthly allotments of cigarettes and sold them on the black market to an Italian gentleman who worked on the base. They sold for $15.00 a carton, a hefty profit for an investment of a dollar-fifty. The problem being that it was illegal and, had they been caught, they might have spent some substantial time in an Italian prison. The next worse thing happened when they sought to make another score. They collected a good quantity of cartons of cigarettes, they had prevailed upon their friends to buy for them, put them in a bag and tossed them over the fence into the waiting arms of the aforementioned Italian gentleman, and they never saw him again. They should have counted themselves lucky but there was not a cool head between them so they went looking for the guy in downtown Catania and ended up being beaten up by several of his friends and family.

Jimmy Watson noticed two Italian men walking arm in arm. The practice is traditional in Italy and no one thinks it anything untoward. But Jimmy was from Paterson, New Jersey and in Paterson, New Jersey men did not walk down the street holding on to each other, unless they were drunk.

"Look at these faggots," Jimmy said, louder than necessary.

Will tried to shush him. "Easy Jimmy, it's apparently okay here. I saw a couple of Italian Navy guys walking like that earlier. I don't think they see anything wrong with it."

"Well they look like fruits to me," Jimmy said. He stopped drawing attention to it but he still looked and chuckled every time he saw two men thusly involved.

"Let's get something to eat," Andy suggested. "John Dolinski told me about a good place to eat called the Rio Ristorante."

"What's that stand for? Jimmy asked.

"River Restaurant," Will said.

"You speak Italian, Will?

"No, but I know a little Spanish and Rio is river in Spanish and Ristorante obviously means restaurant."

"Then you can be our interpreter, can't you," Jimmy

added.

"No," Will said. "I don't know much Spanish and it's not the same anyway."

"We should have brought Dolinski along."

"John ain't Italian, Egg Money, he's Polish," Andy shot back at him.

"Oh," Jimmy said. "It sounds Italian."

"No, it don't," Andy said.

Andy flagged down a cab and asked the driver, "Rio Ristorante?"

The man nodded and motioned for the three of them to get in. They did and he took them to the restaurant on Via Settembre Street. The waiter spoke English so they had no trouble ordering their food. They ordered pizza. The waiter returned about twenty minutes later with the biggest pizza the three of them had ever seen. It looked like pizza you'd get anywhere but it had stuff on it that Will had never seen on pizza. There were slices of hard-boiled eggs, some English peas, and other stuff he did not recognize.

"This is the best damned pizza I ever ate in my life," Jimmy said with his mouth full.

"I have to agree with that, Jimmy," Will said.

Andy nodded and just kept on chewing.

They took a cab back to the base and were up early for a flight. When they returned, Will saw John Dolinski working on one of the planes on another pod, itt was LH-5. He walked over to where John was and asked him if he needed any help.

"We're getting no indication of left gear down when landing." Dolinski said. "They had to fly past the tower so the air controller could look and make sure the wheel was actually down. I've got two guys out sick and this bird has to fly out in the morning. I need to do a gear up check but I need someone to watch the struts for me."

"I'll go get the tug and the APU and the Jacks, Chief,"

Will said.

"I appreciate the help, Will."

Will walked to the hangar, got the key to the Tug, attached the APU (Auxiliary Power Unit) and pulled it out to the pod. He then returned and got Jacks to hold up the plane while they did the gear check. He and Dolinski installed the Jacks and cranked the plane up just enough for the wheels to clear. Then Dolinski climbed aboard and went to the cockpit to operate the gear. Will watched as the gear went up and then as John brought it back down. He noticed that the left gear micro-switch assembly was not anchored properly and was moving when the wheel came down, giving a false indication that the gear was still up. They had to take parts from another airplane that was down for an engine change to replace the ones on the operative plane. They worked till midnight and when Will got back to the barracks he was dead tired but at least he didn't have to fly out the next morning.

About 10:00 am John Dolinski came by Will's bunk and sat down across from him. Will struggled to come awake. He'd been on a twelve-hour hop and then had worked with Dolinski until midnight and his mind was not yet working.

"Hey, John, I mean Chief, what's up?" he said.

"I wanted to come by and thank you for your help last night, Will. It really meant a lot. LH-5 went out on schedule this morning. Not everyone would come off a twelve-hour hop and then jump in and help out the way you did. I won't forget it."

"Anytime you need help, Chief, don't hesitate to ask me. If I'm not in the air, I'll be there to help you."

"That's good to know, Will," Dolinski said. "Oh, and Will."

"Yes Sir, Chief."

"Call me John when it's just the two of us."

Will smiled and nodded.

In late March, Will received a letter from Jamie and sat down on his bunk to read it.

> *Dear Will*
>
> *I have news that I so wanted to share with you in person but since I won't be seeing you again for two more months I had to write you.*
>
> *I've told my parents and all my friends and now I have to tell my baby's daddy. Yes, darling I am pregnant...three months now. I'll be showing in June when you get back.*
>
> *You may not want to have our formal wedding (actually a renewal of our vows). If you don't it will break my heart. Mother says I cannot wear a white dress but that's okay. I'm still glad we got married when we did.*
>
> *I love you, J*

Will was almost catatonic for several days. His joy and excitement morphed into shock and then returned again to joy and excitement. He was going to be a father. It was almost too much to take in. He was twenty-two years old and going to be a family man. He'd always believed it would happen but he'd never thought about how the process would play out.

The crew threw a party for him and even the officers came. They toasted him and congratulated him and patted him on the back. They even started calling him Daddy for a while. Eventually his job brought him back to reality and soon he was looking for ships on the blue Mediterranean trying to keep his mind off Brunswick.

In April, the base started scheduling day trips up Mount Etna. Will and many of the men from VP-21 took advantage of the service and made the trip. The ride up the mountain reminded Will of the Pikes Peak climb he'd been on when he was a kid. His parents took him and his siblings every summer while they were growing up.

The shuttles took them to one of the ski resorts. There was still snow on the mountain in April but it was surprisingly warm. There were many people skiing the slopes and Etna offered a unique experience, that of being able to ski while looking down at the Mediterranean Sea. Some were skiing in short-sleeved shirts due to the higher temperatures in April.

The Navy men drew a lot of attention from the Italians. They bought the men drinks and coffee and wanted to know where each of them was from in the states. When one of the ground crew, a man named Evans, told them he was from Texas they all drew imaginary six-guns and started shooting imaginary bad men with their fingers.

Later they boarded the bus for the ride back down to the base. Will told Jamie about it in the letter he wrote telling her to make arrangements for their 'wedding' in June when he would return from his 'Sicilian vacation'. He wrote to his parents and told them that Jamie would be calling them to let them know when the event would take place.

During this time, a man named Timmons, James Tate, who went by JT did not show up for muster one morning and did not return the next several days. When his body was found in the bottom of a ravine near the base, with several bullet holes in it, a mystery ensued. Sicilian customs and traditions, while seemingly quaint and old fashioned, had played a role in the death of JT Timmons.

The Carabinieri reported that Timmons had likely been

killed by local Mafiosi for taking up with a local girl, which was strictly taboo in rural Sicilian culture. The incident was an eye-opener for many of the Americans who were accustomed to a different set of values and the freedom to pursue happiness, whether permanent or temporary, wherever and whenever they found it. They were warned about getting out of line with local girls lest they end up like 'poor ol' JT did.

Will remembered Timmons as a boorish man who drank too much and possessed an extremely foul mouth. One of the "Fire-watch" guys, duty personnel who patrol the barracks at night to ensure that nothing threatens the safety of the sleeping men, reported finding JT passed out on the toilet one night with his pants still down around his knees, having 'barfed' into the pocket formed by the lowered pants.

It was later discovered that Timmons had bought a motorbike and had ridden it up to Motta, a town on the side of Mount Etna which could be seen from the base. Personnel had been warned about visiting the town because it was purported to be a hotbed of Communist and Mafia activity.

The squadron was told that Timmons had beguiled a young girl from the town and had taken her into Catania for a weekend of illicit activity, this was to the great displeasure of the girl's family and repercussions were extracted from the offender.

ⱷⱷⱷ

Andy Malik wanted to go to Messina, and he wanted Jimmy and Will to go with him. They would need a weekend off in order to have time for the trip. There was a car rental place right across from the base where they could rent a car as long as one of them had an international driver's license. They had two options. First, they could invite the duty driver, a man named Orville Brown who was, according to Jimmy Watson, a fuck-head. "With a name like Orville how could he not be a fuck-head?" Jimmy surmised. The second option was for one of them to get the license. The lot fell on Will because "you're the smartest one of the bunch," Andy told him.

"Ah, flattery works every time," Will said, and agreed to take the class and get the international license. It turned out to be relatively simple. He had to learn all the requisite road signage and Italian vehicle law, who has the right of way in various situations, speed limits of which there didn't seem to be any. In a week's time Will was legal to drive in Italy.

They rented a 1962 Fiat 500, mustard yellow and about the size of a sardine can, with only one saving grace, it got almost forty miles to a gallon of gas. The cars were obviously built to carry around the smaller framed Italians and no consideration had been given to the typically larger Americans. Will, at 5'11" was extremely cramped and Andy and Jimmy, only a couple inches shorter than Will were not any less restricted in their movement and flexibility in the tiny car. The car was fast though and it climbed the hills with apparent ease as they headed up the coast highway toward Messina.

At Taormina, they decided to have lunch and explore the picturesque town. It was built in terraces up the side of the mountains that came right down to the sea. It was the most beautiful place he'd ever seen, Will thought and he was already planning in his head to return one day with his family, the one now being formed back in Brunswick.

"What would you guys like to have for lunch?" Will asked the other two.

"Let's try some Italian food, "Jimmy said, from the back seat.

"Well, you're in luck, my good man," Will responded,

"this place is crawling with Italian restaurants."

They spotted a place conspicuously named *Ristorante Pizzeria Santini* and Will pulled into the parking lot. "This looks like a good place," he said.

"Why not," Andy said.

The waiter was surly and obviously did not like Americans. He was slow about coming over to take their order.

"You having a bad day, Pablo?" Jimmy asked the man, who appeared not to understand what he had said.

"I don't think his name is Pablo, Jimmy," Andy said.

"Try not to piss him off any more than he is already," Will cautioned them. "I don't want spit in my food."

Whether the man did not speak English or was pretending not to be able to speak any English, Will was not prepared to say. It might have been unusual for a waiter in a restaurant in such an internationally known tourist resort as Taormina, to not know English, but the three of them didn't find anything disconcerting about it.

They ordered cokes and the man repeated "Coca Cola" and left the table. He returned in about ten minutes with the drinks then got out his pad to take their food order. Unable to read the menu they just ordered Spaghetti and meatballs which to Americans is the cheeseburger and fries of the Italian diet.

The man returned twenty minutes later and told them, "No spaghetti."

"It took you twenty minutes to figure out you're out of fucking spaghetti?" Andy Malik said to him.

"No spaghetti," the man repeated.

They asked for the menu again and the waiter brought it to them, they decided to order Ravioli this time. The man wrote down their order and was turning to go when Andy called to him.

"Hey, Garcon," he said, and motioned for the man to come over to him. The man approached him.

"Listen Pal." Andy said, looking him right in the eye. "I don't know if you can understand what I'm saying or not but if you come back here in twenty minutes, and tell me you're out of Ravioli, I'm going to whip your Ginny ass."

The Ravioli came and to Will's surprise and relief there didn't appear to be any rat turds or pubic hair in any of their meals. Three hours later, on the continued journey up the coast to Messina, they had not gotten sick from food poisoning nor had they died from arsenic in their lunch.

"I guess that fucker did understand some English," Jimmy commented. "I was sure looking forward to watching you whip his ass, Andy."

"Remember in Ceiba when Dawson cracked that guy in the head with his pool stick?" Will said.

"Yeah, they came out of the woodwork, everyone in the place came after us for that." Jimmy replied. "And the same thing would have happened today probably if Andy had really started kicking the guy's ass."

"Well wouldn't you do that back home, if a foreigner started pounding on another American?" Will asked.

"Not if he started the shit, then it's a self-inflicted wound," Jimmy said. "That time at Joe and Nino's in Portland, when Sam Kinney cut in on those two lesbians dancing, he was after the lipstick lesbian, and the "man" of the two knocked Sam on his ass, none of us went to help him out, we just laughed our asses off."

'Now that's loyalty," Andy said.

"But really," Jimmy countered. "If some guy is being an asshole, American or otherwise, I'm under no obligation to help bail his ass out of a jam."

They found a hotel in Messina that had been recommended by one of the guys at the base because it was cheap. They rented three rooms for two days, each of which had a bed and not much else. A common bathroom was at the end of the hall. It was austere but comfortable enough. The next day, Saturday, they toured Messina. Jimmy tried talking up the few girls they came across without chaperones but he had no luck. Will and Andy were getting the smiles but that was as far as it went.

The city, as was Taormina, was terraced up the side of the mountains that came down to the sea. It was a beautiful city, similar to Catania, but not like Taormina which seemed more placid and aloof. At the harbor, you could look across the Strait of Messina and see the 'toe' of the Italian boot, mainland Italy, about three miles across the strait.

Strait of Messina seen from the hill of "Pentimele," near Reggio Calabria. In the distance is snow covered Mount Etna

There were hydrofoils traversing the strait between Messina and the mainland ferrying people from Messina and Villa San Giovanni as well as between Messina and Reggio Calabria.

A girl who spoke perfect English, with no Italian accent approached Will and started a conversation. She'd heard them talking about Messina. "You guys are navy, right?"

"Yes," Will responded, "we're on deployment at Sigonella."

"I thought so," she said and continued telling him about the history of Messina and Sicily in general. The other two noticed and came over to join in. The girl was more than happy to educate them and she seemed to know everything about just about everything. She invited them to a small coffee shop near the harbor and they followed her. They found a table and sat down. She asked them what they wanted and ordered in Italian.

"You speak perfect English, how did that happen?" Will asked her.

"I'm American," she said. "Italian American, my family is from Connecticut. My name is Jessie Bonetti, I had to learn Italian. My father insisted I learn it so I could do advanced studies here in Messina. His family was from Messina. I go to the University of Messina."

"I'm Will Cain, I'm from Colorado originally but for the time being my home is in Maine where my squadron is stationed. These two fellows are my good friends and crewmates, Andy Malik and Jimmy Watson. The girl showed no indication that she had even heard the names of the other two. Jimmy tilted his head to stick his nose up to suggest that she was 'stuck up'.

She was beautiful but Will refused to let himself be distracted by it. While Andy and Jimmy were choking on their tongues, he was maintaining a cordial conversation with her and not just pretending to be interested in what she had to say. He found her intelligence refreshing and fascinating.

She paid for the coffee and the various pies and cakes she'd ordered. She continued her conversing with Will as the other two just looked on, smiling at him then at her and then at each other. Will knew that she was ignoring them and he started to get uncomfortable.

"When are you going back to your base?" she asked him.

"In the morning," he said.

"I have an apartment near here. You can come and stay with me tonight and I can teach you a lot more about the history of Sicily," she said, looking him intently in the eyes. She glanced at the other two and quickly added, "but it's a very small apartment, I only have one bed."

Andy tapped Jimmy on the shoulder. "Come on, Jimmy," he said. Let's go. Give me the key to the car, Will, we'll meet you right here in the morning, Okay?"

"No, hold on Andy," he said, "give me just a minute here, don't leave." They said they'd wait at the car and walked off toward the harbor.

"Listen, Jessie," he began, "you're a beautiful girl, one of the prettiest girls I think I've ever seen."

"But," she said, "you're married."

He sighed. "Yes I am." How did you know?"

"You've got married written all over your face. I was just hoping I was getting false signals."

"I've got a baby on the way and I am in love with his mother."

"She's a lucky girl to have such a faithful man, and such a handsome man. You realize that I had no intention of giving you a history lesson, don't you?"

"Oh God," he said, sighing again, "please don't make this any harder than it already is."

"I won't, Will," she told him and held out her hand, "I enjoyed the conversation. Good luck to you."

He shook her hand, "thanks for the history lesson and for everything else."

He was glad that Andy and Jimmy were with him because he feared that he might not have been able to resist jumping into bed with such a lovely creature who had made him an offer not many men would have, or could have, walked away from. Regardless, it was done, and he went to find his two friends.

"You pussy," Jimmy yelled at him when he got back to the car. "Why can't shit like that happen to me sometimes?"

"Because you look like a finger-puppet, that's why, you red-headed prick." Andy said, laughing.

"One day, my friend," Andy told him," you're going to look back on this day and kick your own ass for not spending the night with that woman."

"Maybe," Will said," but I hope not. I don't want any dishonesty in my marriage. I don't ever want to hurt Jamie."

"I admire that quality in you, Will," Andy replied, "Don't understand it but admire it just the same."

"I don't," Jimmy threw in, "I think he's a pussy but I still love him.

e౧౬౧

In May, they participated in Project Mercury, as a Launch/Recover unit for Astronaut Gordon Cooper. It was their final mission in Sicily.

On June 1, 1963, LH-12 lifted off the runway at Sigonella for the last time. They made a brief stop in the Azores for rest and refueling and then touchdown at Brunswick on the third.

CHAPTER 9

Clare

Jamie and the baby were waiting for him when he climbed out of LH-12 just as she said she would be. "You're putting on some weight, I see," he told her. "I've got a bump alright. You may not like me when I get fatter."

"That won't happen, not liking you I mean. How did your folks take the news about the baby?"

"They were ecstatic about it, Daddy is happy to become a grandfather. And Mother is just happy her grandbaby was not conceived out of wedlock.

"I am too," he said. "I'm glad we got married, Jamie. I love calling you my wife and not just my girlfriend. You're beautiful, by the way."

"Daddy says I have that glow women get when they're pregnant."

"You've always had that glow to me," he said. So, how's the little guy doing?"

"He or she is doing just fine, I'm due in September, sometime around the end of the month. I guess that last night before you left was the money shot."

"I couldn't be happier, Jamie, it's like a dream come true. The guys threatened to throw me out of the plane if I didn't stop grinning all the time. So, when's the 'wedding'?"

"June fifteenth at the First Parish Church. You know that big church you drive around going back to the base."

"Yes," he said. "I'll have to buy a suit, I don't even own a suit. I might get married in uniform."

"That's a minor problem. You can rent one if you have to. I like the uniform idea. I talked to your folks, in fact I talked to everyone in the family, they're coming a few days early. We'll have to pick them up in Portland. They're getting a motel room."

"I've got so much to tell you about where I've been. We have to go back to Italy one day. I mean I have to take you to the places I've been. It's so beautiful there, you'll love it."

"I wish I could have been there with you," she said. "I missed you so much. I went to Land's End just about every weekend and pretended you were there with me."

"I hope nobody saw you talking to me when I wasn't there."

They were kissing between sentences.

"I don't 'think' anybody saw me," she said, smiling.

"I'm taking a week's leave for the wedding. I already got it approved and they were very good to let me tell them which days I need when I got back. I don't want to go anywhere, I just want to hang around town. We do need to find a place to live."

"We can stay with my parents if you don't mind, Will. That way I can walk to work and Mother can take me to class at night. You'll need the car to get to the base and…but it's up to you."

"Let me think about it. That sounds good but I'd love to have time alone with just you and the baby."

"I'll live in a hovel if we have to."

"We may have to, on my pay, but I want what's best for all of us," he said. "I'm going to ask Jimmy Watson to be my Best Man, if you have no objection."

"That's Egg Money?"

"Yes, but we don't call him that much anymore since Sam died. Sam gave him that name and I think Jimmy was really close to Sam. Sam helped Jimmy get on crew. Even after Jimmy went to A School for Radioman, he still had a hard time because he's not very smart and he's kind of goofy acting sometimes."

"I have no objection," she said.

Will's folks arrived at the Portland Airport on the thirteenth of June and Will and Jamie were there to pick them up. They'd borrowed the Dunham's car because Will's Ford Falcon could not carry them all along with their luggage.

It was a long-awaited meeting for all of them. Will and Jamie were waiting for them when they got off the concourse.

"You look like your father," Jamie said, as the four Cains approached. "Your letters didn't do her Justice, Will," his father said. "She's beautiful just like you said but I had no idea she was this beautiful. Jamie was appropriately cordial. She was accustomed to compliments but sometimes older men tended to overdo it. Bill Cain meant well but he impressed her as being a little uncomfortable with her.

"We are so glad to finally meet you, dear, Ellen Cain said and hugged her tightly, "you're everything Will said you were."

Will's sister seemed to hit it off with Jamie right away, and he could envision their being friends. His brother, Tommy however was dumbstruck and was unable to say much. "She's really pretty, Will," was all he said.

She thought they might be prudes, except for the sister, and were maybe nervous about meeting her. Will assured her that his folks were not prudes. "They're just social outcasts who don't get along well with real people." He said.

"Nuh-uh, you know that's not true," she said. "They seem very nice, it's just awkward meeting one's in-laws. Maine will seem like a foreign country to them I imagine"

"It did to me when I first got here, but it grows on you."

Bill's father had made reservations at a motel in Portland and had rented a car so they could spend a day or two seeing the state. None of them, except for Bill, had ever been out of Colorado, except to Wyoming and New Mexico a few times. Bill had been all over the West Coast and all over the Pacific during the war, but that was not much like a vacation.

"I brought the Dunham's car so we could fit everyone in. You didn't have to rent a car."

"It'll be easier for everyone," he said. "It's really good to see you, Son, and your girl is wonderful."

"Thanks, Dad, Will responded and he hugged them all before he and Jamie left to drive back to Brunswick. "My folks are a little standoffish at first. My dad will lighten up when he meets your folks. They have a lot to talk about."

"They're nice, Will, especially your sister. She's what, eighteen?"

"Twenty," Will said, "Tommy is eighteen."

"He's shy, isn't he?"

"No, I think he was tongue-tied over you. His jaw dropped when he saw you."

"I don't believe that," she said.

"Why not? Mine did too."

Jamie's mother helped her pick out a beige dress for her wedding. Being a slender girl she had a pronounced baby bump but not a huge bump and they selected a dress that covered it as much as was possible. The pastor was asked to explain the situation that this event was a renewal of vows since the actual wedding had taken place a year earlier and, due to Will's deployment there had not been enough time to have a formal wedding.

Sarah Miller, Jamie's friend from high school, and her family were there along with many others from their high school class. Betty the waitress had been invited because, as Will had said, "This would not be happening if it hadn't been for Betty."

Will had invited his crew but didn't really expect them all to show up. He was wrong because every one of them came decked out in their best 'dress whites', even the Officers. He had not fully understood just how close air crewmembers really were to each other until they formed a 'gauntlet' down the aisle for Jamie and her father to walk through on their way to their husband and son-in-law waiting at the front of the church.

Sarah Miller was Jamie's maid of honor and Jimmy Watson, spiffy in his dress white uniform and dixie cup, stood beside Will, who had decided to get married in uniform as well. At the reception Will thanked Lieutenant Powell, and the rest of the crew, for coming in full regalia. "It was a really nice touch," he told them.

"Chief Dolinski has suggested a man to fly with us until you come back from leave," the Lieutenant told him. "He's a Striker for crewmember and he can use the experience."

"It's only for a week," Will said, "I'll be back."

"Enjoy your honeymoon, Will, your bride is a lovely girl, excuse me a lovely woman."

They decided, after Jamie's urging, to go to Quebec for their honeymoon but would leave the next morning after spending time with Will's family before they departed. The Dunhams had them for dinner the night before they were to leave.

Bill Cain talked to his son about coming home when his hitch was up. His argument was compelling and Will listened with an open mind.

"I really hope you don't decide to make the navy a career," he said. "The military will ruin your life, Will. They own you and they come first ahead of your wife and kids and family. It's really disruptive to everyone in your life."

"But you've always gone on about the marines, how you are proud to have been in the marines."

"And I am proud but that was a different time and situation. We were at war and the threat to a country at war has to take priority over everything. I'm proud of what I did but I don't want my son's life disrupted the way mine was, not ever."

"I've thought about it, Dad," Will said. "I love the flying but eventually I could end up on a Carrier and never get back home. I think the thought of not being there when my son or daughter is growing up is just something I can't comprehend."

"I hope you'll come home when you get out and come and work with me in the business. I'm forty-seven and not getting any younger. I know that's a cliché but it is true. We have a few years for you to learn the business and one day it will be yours to run. It will give you the means to provide for your family the way you want to, and the way I know you believe they deserve."

"Okay, Dad, I'll think seriously about it."

At the airport, Will hugged his mother. "I love you Mom," he said, "and I miss you."

"I love you too, Honey," Ellen Cain said. "I hope you come home before I get so fat you can't get your arms around me to hug me like that again."

"You're not fat, Mom, you're pleasantly plump."

"That's what they always say."

"We'll it's true," he told her.

He hugged his sister, Julie and his brother Tommy. "You're beautiful, Julie," he said, "and Tommy, it looks like you might be taller than me before too long."

Everybody hugged Jamie and told her they were proud to have her in the family.

The New England aloofness of the Dunham family mixed well with the more openness of the Western personalities, despite Will's concern about that before the meeting of the two, and the two patriarchs, with their common history in the military and in the war, hit it off well. Richard Dunham promised Bill Cain that he'd come to Colorado and hunt deer in the Rockies after "the kids" were out of the Navy.

The drive to Quebec was an experience in itself for Will. Up through Waterville, Skowhegan and along Route 201 beside the Kennebec River was some of the most beautiful country he'd ever seen, not discounting that he was a son of the Rockies. Across the Canadian border through Saint Georges, Beauceville and across the St. Lawrence River into Quebec City, he marveled at the lush greenery of the entire state of Maine and the country of Canada.

"I never would have seen all this without you, Jamie. I would have missed it. My gosh what a wonderful place you grew up in. Can you leave this and come to Colorado with me?

"Yes Will, I can, and I will—Will," she said, laughing.

"Okay, I can see we are starting a family tradition," he told her, and laughed too. "Have your fun, nothing is going to upset me this week."

"I'll stop doing that if you really want me too."

"No don't stop, I think it's funny."

"Good thing you're not from the south or I'd call you Billy Joe."

"Billy Joe?" he said quizzically.

"William Joseph, Billy Joe," she explained.

"Oh, I hadn't thought of that. And it's a good thing you

are not from the south or they'd probably be calling you Jamie Lou."

Quebec City, Ville Quebec as Jamie pronounced, showing off her limited command of French, was the most beautiful city he'd ever seen, Will decided. It was even more beautiful than Londonderry, and Messina. The city was captivating. There were sidewalk cafes and parks where artists were selling their work and so much to see he didn't think they could see it all in only a week.

Skyline of Ville Quebec

In Vieux Quebec, Voo Kebec, as Jamie said it was pronounced, they visited the Chateau Frontenac, a grand hotel that first opened in 1893, and walked along the boardwalk that overlooked the St. Lawrence River and the port below.

"We'll come back here one day and stay in that hotel," he told her, "but for now the motel will have to do."

At the Citadel, they watched the Changing of the Guard which, as the brochure they got at the entry told them, had been a tradition since 1928. It was performed in traditional uniforms by members of the Royal 22e Regiment of the Canadian Regular Force. It was a unique event in Quebec, inspired by the Changing of the Royal Guard in England.

The full-dress uniforms consisted of, among other things, a scarlet tunic and a bearskin hat, and attested to the authenticity of the ceremony. It is conducted only in England and Canada.

Will noticed that, at one segment of their march, the soldiers would take a step and slide their foot a short distance before putting it down. They did this for the full extent of the parade ground. He wondered if it had any special meaning or significance but no one he asked seemed to know.

On the outer wall, they found a bench and sat for over an hour, without uttering a word, looking at the panorama of the city, the Chateau Frontenac and many ships docked on the river below. He eventually broke the silence.

"So much has happened to me, Jamie, in the past three years. I feel like I've lived my entire life since I came to Maine. Nothing that happened to me before then matters much to me."

"I feel the same way," she said. "Since I met you, my life has started to make sense. We're going to have a baby, Will, can you believe that?"

He nodded, "Sometimes I almost start bawling just thinking about it. I hope it's a girl who'll grow up to look just like you."

"A girl you say, why not a boy who looks like you?"

"That would be okay too," he said.

"What will we name our baby if it's a boy?"

"I have an idea for a boy or a girl, but you'll think it's crazy."

"No I won't, what is it?"

"Well," he said, "if it's a boy I'd like to name him Jamie."

"Oh, and I suppose if it's girl you want to name her Will?"

"No, I'd like to name her Clare after the place we met."

"Oh, my gosh, Will, I love it. That is so cool. Let's do it."

"You like it?"

"Yes," she said, putting her hands up to her cheeks, "yes indeed. Can we name her middle name Marie? That's my mother's middle name."

"Anything you want, I like that. Clare Marie Cain, yes it has a ring to it, doesn't it?"

"It does, I think it's beautiful," she said.

"Then we should hope for a girl, I've always wanted to have a daughter," he told her.

The week was too quickly over and routine again became a way of life for both of them. Part of the squadron was sent to Key West for a couple of months but thankfully LH-12 was not one of the crews that had to go.

Will was starting to think about what he would do to make a living if he did not stay in the Navy. He'd pretty much decided not to take that course. Jamie was against it although she was not pushing him to get out when his time was up. He could tell she really didn't want to be alone with the baby for extended periods of time while he was on deployment. He didn't want that either.

On September 24, 1963, he made his decision. He was in the waiting room of the Maternity Ward of the base hospital, with Richard Dunham while their daughter and wife was giving birth to her first child.

June Dunham had stayed with her daughter throughout her labor and birth. She went to tell the men.

"It's a girl," she shouted as she walked into the waiting room and the three of them hugged each other exuberantly.

"How are they doing?" Will asked her.

"It was not an easy delivery, Will," she said. It was a long labor, as you know and Jamie is a very small girl, you know, in the hips I mean."

"Can I see them?" A nurse led him into the room where they had placed the baby next to Jamie on the bed. Jamie was worn out and looked like she had been run through a wringer.

"I'm okay," she told him, "just very tired. But she's here now so I won't curse you out, maybe later I might.

"It's okay if you want to curse me out, I'll take it like a

man," he told her. He picked up his new daughter and held her close to his chest. "Nothing ever felt like this, nothing in my life ever felt like this." Then he kissed Jamie and hugged her and the baby until the Dunhams came into the room to see their new granddaughter.

"I want to go to my room," Jamie said.

"But this is your room, dear," her mother replied.

"No, my room at home, I want to go home."

They made a nursery for baby Clare out of the spare bedroom on the second floor and June took care of her until Jamie could get back on her feet. A month after the baby was born Jamie suffered an attack of postpartum depression that lasted three months. She seemed sad and listless and was overly contentious with everyone, especially with Will. He was starting to wish for a deployment to get him away from her until she got through it.

In November, a national tragedy would only add to their turmoil. On the twenty-second Will and Jimmy Watson were walking from the VP-21 hangar to an office on the base to take care of some personal business when a friend of theirs in another squadron yelled out the barracks window at them. "Hey Will, did you hear the President's been shot.

"No shit?" Jimmy yelled back, "is he okay?"

"Don't know, the man said shrugging his shoulders.

"Where did it happen?" Will asked him.

"It was somewhere in Texas, Dallas, I think it was."

They arrived at their destination and the two women working in the office were listening intently to the radio. Then the voice of Walter Cronkite came on again.

> *"From Dallas, Texas, the flash, apparently official: President Kennedy died at 1 p.m. Central Standard Time. 2 o'clock Eastern Standard Time, some 38 minutes ago."*

One of the women let out a scream and both broke into sobs. Will and Jimmy just stood there stunned and dumbstruck, not knowing what to do. "Come on, Jimmy, we can come back another day," Will said, and they left the office and returned to the hangar where it was like a dead zone. The workday was almost over so those who did not have duty were told to take off and that they would be notified if they were needed.

Will drove home to the Dunhams house where the somber mood prevailed there as well. The family loved John Kennedy and their hurt was deep and painful. Disbelief was the predominant emotion. No one could even imagine how such a thing could happen. The loss of the president they loved and admired only worsened Jamie's depression. She cried a lot and sat for hours without speaking. But by Christmas she was feeling better and was up and around showing new life. She started taking care of the baby and involving herself in the family again.

"I'm glad to have you back, Baby," Will said.

"I'm sorry, it must have been awful for you. I don't know what came over me," she replied.

"I'm not going to stay in the Navy, Jamie."

"Oh Will, I'm so happy you decided that. I've been terrified you'd have to go away again."

"Well now we have to consider what to do from here on out."

"I can teach school."

"That's okay if it's what you want to do but I have to earn a living. I have to support my family, you and Clare."

"What do 'you' want to do? Whatever it is I'll go along with it."

"I'm torn between two things here," he told her. "I promised your father I wouldn't take you away unless he thinks it's best for us. But I really think I'd like to go home."

"Then let's do it, Will, let's go to Colorado. You don't have a problem working for your dad, do you?"

"My heart tells me I should do things on my own without his help, but my head tells me it's the best thing for us."

"I want to go home with you and raise our daughter in Colorado. If your concern is taking us away from Maine, then dismiss that concern. Staying here because of some misguided sense of duty, and a promise made to my father is not what I want. And it's not what he wants either."

Will nodded up and down slowly, in deep thought about what she had said, and then kissed her hand. "Thank you, Honey," he said. I just needed to know it's what you really want. Then that's it, we'll do it."

CHAPTER 10

Contract Lost

In the middle of January 1964, It was one month until Will's enlistment was up. Excitement was running high in the Cain and Dunham household. The Dunhams, Richard and June were saddened to know their daughter, granddaughter and son-in-law would be leaving them, ostensibly forever. There would be the occasional visit at Christmas or Thanksgiving, of course, but in practical terms, they would be out of their lives forever. It was the way of the world, June Dunham intimated to herself, when you have a daughter, she's going to get married one day and leave you. If she marries her high school sweetheart, hopefully she will move across town. If she marries a military man she may move across the country. At least her daughter met and married a good man that she loves and they have baby girl they love as much as they love each other. June Dunham would spend many sleepless hours, in the coming months, crying herself to sleep at night.

As traumatic as the departure of their daughter and her family would be for them, the Dunhams were happy and full of hope for their future in their new home in Colorado. Their lives were rich with opportunity and optimism. It reminded Richard Dunham of those exciting and anticipatory days when he came home from the war in Europe. It was a time of great promise in which Americans felt like anything and everything they did and wanted to do would be successful and blessed. Richard had never lost that inner joy and belief, that everything was always right in and for The United States, until President Kennedy was killed. The wind just sort of went out of him on that day and he never got it back. Now a young man would be taking his daughter and his granddaughter out of his life, and he knew it was for their own good. He was thankful to Will Cain although the pain was almost unbearable.

Two weeks before he would leave the Navy forever, LH-12 was scheduled for one last mission. "One more trip out over the pond, baby," he told Jamie, "and it'll all be over.

"I'm so happy, Will, I can't wait to get on the road. I've been looking forward to this ever since we decided to do it. It just seemed like the time would never come."

After the aircraft crossed the coast and headed out into the Atlantic, Lieutenant Powell came on the intercom. "Let me have your attention, please," he said. "As most of you are aware, this is AE-2 Will Cain's farewell tour. He will be leaving the navy, Combat Aircrew Twelve and all his buddies, who have watched out for him and taken care of him for all these years." Groans went up all over the aircraft.

Will clicked his mic from his position in the nose bubble. "Thank you for the guilt trip, Skipper," he said.

"Just wanted to let you know how much we'll miss you, Cain."

"Thank you, Sir. I'll miss everyone too, but the mountains are calling me back home."

"Egg Money, you better not be bawling," Andy called out to Jimmy Watson.

"I'm not bawling." Watson responded, "but dammit to hell." He clicked off the intercom.

Three hours later they were six-hundred miles from land and making a wide circle, having dropped one sono-buoy and were listening for activity below sea. Will was poised in his chair in the forward observation station, with his binoculars held up to his eyes, combing the sea surface for any sign of shipping. It was quiet, very quiet and he hoped it would remain quiet. His thoughts now were on home and on getting his family settled into their new life. He noticed some dark clouds forming off to the northwest just as Egg Money reported that Brunswick Control was informing them that a line of thunder storms was producing some activity between 'Broomstick' and their position. Lieutenant Powell announced that they were going to call it a day and head home.

"We've got foul weather in our way on the flight path home so we're turning around," he said, over the intercom. "Everybody relax. it's no big deal but we don't want to get caught this far out in rough weather."

The ship turned and began to lumber northwest toward home base and the approaching storms. Powell considered flying around the storms but Brunswick told him they extended too far south and it would take too much fuel. They would have to fly through the weather.

"Port engine is heating up," the co-pilot reported. Powell looked at the gauge on the dashboard.

"Shit, what's going on with that. Go take a look Andy." He said to Andy Malik.

Malik got up and went back to the flight deck side window and looked out at the port engine. "I don't see anything externally wrong with the engine, Skipper," he told Lieutenant Powell when he got back to the cockpit.

"Okay," Powell said. "Thank you. "Keep an eye on it, Kyle, and let me know if it gets worse." Just as he said that, they felt a shudder in the aircraft and heard a loud clunk in the engine.

"That sounded like we threw a piston." Andy said.

"That's what I was thinking too," Powell replied, "Better shut it down, Kyle."

"Shutting down and feathering," Murphy responded as he made the necessary adjustments.

"Well, this throws a kink in the works, guys." Powell said. "Now we're going to have to fight the storm on one engine. It's no big deal but just a bit of a pain in the neck. I'd better let the crew know our status.

"Listen up," Powell said over the intercom. "We've lost number one engine so we're heading for home but we're going to have to go through some pretty rough weather on the way. We may be able to go over it but it's doubtful with only one engine. Tie down any loose equipment and I want every man in a life vest just in case."

That was surely not as ominous as it sounded, Will was thinking from his position in the bubble, but he retrieved his life vest and put it on anyway. It was about an hour before the lightning started and rain started pelting the Plexiglas around him. In a short time, he couldn't see out of the aircraft, not even a few feet. He called the pilot.

"Request permission to vacate the bubble, Skipper. I can't see anything past the glass."

"Yes, go ahead, Cain," Powell said. "See if you can help secure any loose equipment in the rear."

"Yes Sir, Mister Powell, thank you." He crawled back along the tunnel and climbed up to the flight deck, then he slid over the wing beam to the Radio Shack where Jimmy Watson was busy on his headset. In the back of the aircraft, the others had used bungie cables to secure tool boxes and other items that might go flying around in the unlikely event they had to ditch.

"You guys need any help?" Will asked Larry Dawson.

"Nah, we're good," Dawson said. "It's a hell of a last flight for you, ain't it, Will?

"Yeah, it is. I wasn't looking for any excitement, I just wanted to get it over with and go home."

"Don't worry, these are tough old birds. We'll get you back in one piece, alive"

"Thanks for adding 'alive' at the end, Larry," Will said, and they both laughed.

Suddenly the aircraft began to be pummeled by high wind and rain. It began to roll severely, Will and Dawson had to grab hold of structural members in order to steady themselves. Lieutenant Powell's voice came on the intercom.

"We're entering the front wall of the storm so all hands find secure seating and steady yourselves and hold on while until we get through this."

It was a mad few minutes as LH-12 rolled and pitched dramatically. Will had never experienced such turbulence before in any aircraft. The Neptunes rarely encountered such heavy weather. The Ordinance man, Gerald Lowery, was in the port-side observation station and Dawson was in the Starboard chair so Will went up to the Radio Shack where Jimmy Watson was frantically tapping out Morse Code messages. Will sat down and leaned back against the wing beam and pressed his feet against the back bulkhead. Watson was shouting profanities at every clap of thunder that shook the aircraft. It would have been funny to Will, had it not been so scary.

It became calm for a short time and LH-12 smoothed out and everyone dared to breathe a sigh of relief but Powell warned them not to relax.

"It's not over, gentlemen," he said. "We're heading into another wall in just a few minutes. Stay alert and don't anyone walk around."

The aircraft started pitching again and the wind and rain resumed even harder than before. All of a sudden there was a loud crack, like an explosion, and the interior of the plane lit up as bright as day. A flash traveled the length of the cabin along the skin. The Ship shuddered and felt as if it was going to stall.

"What the hell was that?" Dawson yelled into his mic.

"Lightning hit the number two engine." Powell told them. "It's lost, I've got the jets on. Hopefully we can get to sunshine with just the jets. Prepare to ditch just in case."

Will was in a daze. Here he was with less than two weeks left in the Navy and they may end up in the ocean, several hundred miles from home. What a hell of a way to end his hitch.

"I've lost my trailing wire, Skipper, we got no long-range radio." Egg Money reported to Lieutenant Powell.

"Dammit," Powell said. "Okay, Watson, there's nothing we can do about that now. When was the last time you reported our position to Brunswick?"

"About two minutes ago, Skipper." Jimmy said.

"Okay, thank you."

Powell assessed their situation. "I don't want to ditch in the weather but I don't think we can get out of it on the jets. If we go down here, the Coast Guard is going to have a hard time finding us."

"We're losing altitude, Art," Kyle Murphy told him.

"I know, let's wait a few more minutes. I want to do this under control. Can you see how rough the water is down there?"

Murphy looked out his window for about 30 seconds. "Swells look to be about thirty feet and maybe two-hundred feet apart."

"Okay," Powell nodded, "Here's the plan, and I'll inform the crew in a minute. I'll set down between the swells, at least that's what I'll attempt. Andy, you go back and release the raft as soon as the aircraft comes to stop. Hustle the men up. When the men in the back are out, you go out, don't mess around. You get your ass out of this airplane as fast as you can."

"Yes Sir, Captain, I got it." Andy said.

Powell apprised the crew of the plan to ditch and turned the aircraft on a heading toward the coast of Maine. He shut down the two jet engines just as the plane went over a swell and skimmed along the surface of the water. It plunged into another swell but went through it without any apparent trouble. It came to rest just as another swell past through them then Powell yelled to Andy Malik to eject the life raft. Andy did as he was ordered and then started yelling.

"Everybody out of the plane, everybody out."

Will and Dawson and Lowery went out the back, port window and swam to the raft that Andy had released. They climbed onto the wing and held the raft until the others had exited the plane and were boarding the raft. Lieutenant Powell was the last man to get into the raft. Will looked around and started counting noses.

"Where's Jimmy?" he yelled. "Jimmy's not here." They all looked around but Jimmy Watson could not be seen.

Will started climbing out of the raft and Lieutenant Powell yelled at him over the wind and rain.

"Sit back down, Will," he said, "don't leave this raft."

"But he's my best friend, Skipper," Will yelled back. "I have to go find him"

Powell grabbed Will's life vest and pulled him close to his face. "Son, you've got a week left in the navy, I'm not going to tell your family that I let you go back into a sinking airplane and drown. I'm not going to lose both of you today. You keep your ass in this raft. That's an order. Do you understand me?"

"Yes Sir, Mister Powell," Will said, and he sat back down.

With that said, Powell plunged out of the raft and

started swimming toward the aircraft. When he was almost to the wing, Jimmy Watson popped up from under the fuselage of the airplane. Powell saw him and swam to him and helped him to the raft. Some of the guys pulled him into it and were patting him on the back.

"What the hell happened to you, Watson?" Powell asked him when they were all settled in.

I went out the wrong window and had to swim under the plane to get over here," Jimmy told them.

"You, dumb fuck." Dawson yelled at him. "What if it had sunk on top of you?"

"I never thought about that," Jimmy said, sheepishly. They didn't see the plane sink below the waves. The swells carried them away from it too quickly.

Night came and the storm passed over them. Dawson had the foresight to bring some canned goods along with him when he went overboard so they wouldn't starve to death, at least not for a day or so.

"They know our most recent position. They'll be out looking for us."

The sea was relatively calm so a few of the men were able to get some sleep despite the fact that they were wet and cold.

Back in Brunswick, the Squadron Commander and FAW-3 (Fleet Air Wing-3) Commander were in the operations room, coordinating the search and rescue operation. At first light, navy personnel started notifying the families of LH-12 crewmembers who lived in the area.

The trauma of receiving such a phone call is known only to very few people but it is something not soon forgotten. When Jamie Cain picked up the phone that morning, her world seemed to fall in on her. She was almost catatonic. Her mother implored her. "What's wrong, Honey? What has happened?" But Jamie could not speak. June Dunham started sobbing and called her husband.

Richard came into the kitchen where his daughter was holding the phone, in shock. He took it from her. "This is Richard Dunham. I'm Jamie's father, can you tell me what has happened?"

"Yes, sir, Mister Dunham, this is Yeoman 2nd, Matt Kelly at NAS Brunswick. LH-12 encountered heavy weather about four-hundred miles off the coast and has disappeared from the radar screen. As a precaution, we are notifying the families of crewmembers who live in the immediate area."

"Thank you, Mister Kelly, I appreciate that," Richard said. "Can you tell me what efforts are being made to locate the aircraft?"

"The Coast Guard went out from the South Portland facility this morning before dawn and every squadron here at Brunswick has launched at least one flight out for search and rescue. Right now, there are fifteen or twenty aircraft from up and down the coast out looking. We are confident we'll find them."

"Can we come to the base and wait for any news there?

"I'll ask and see if I can get authorization for that and call you back in just a few."

"Thank you, son, we'll be grateful to you."

June was holding on to Jamie, who was weeping uncontrollably. Richard went to her and took her into his arms. "Honey, they're doing everything they can. They have the Coast Guard out and aircraft from all up and down the coast searching for them. I won't tell you not to worry because I know you will but just don't despair."

"I can't lose him, Daddy," she said through her tears. "He has a week left, one week, and this happens. Oh God, this can't be happening. We have a baby who might not ever know her daddy."

"The man on the phone is going to call back in a while and tell us if we can come to the base and wait there for news of the rescue operations. Do you want to do that?"

Jamie nodded her head. "Yes, I'd like to be there."

They received a return call from Yeoman Kelly advising them that they had authorization to come to the base and follow the search and rescue operations. June Dunham decided to stay at home with the baby.

When Richard and Jamie arrived at the entrance gate, the Marine on duty had prior notification they would be arriving. He gave them a special card for their car and directions to the NAS operations facility. An officer from VP-21 met them and led them to a waiting room.

"I'm Lieutenant Commander Jeff Woodson," he told them. "You should be comfortable in here. There is coffee and some snacks. I will keep you informed of any development I hear just as soon as I know. I know it's useless to tell you not to worry, we're all worried. But we are confident that the crew would have ditched and gotten into the life raft. It's just a matter of time before we find them. So please, just be cautiously optimistic."

Thank you, Commander," Richard said, "We appreciate your concern. My daughter is pretty distraught."

"I understand but try and comfort her. We're going to find those men and bring them home."

In the raft at sea, Dawson was opening up canned goods and passing them around.

"Is green beans and carrots all you got?" Andy Malik yelled. "What the hell kind of a café is this?"

"When was the last time you swam in freezing water with a box of canned veggies under one arm, Malik?" Dawson responded. "Hand me that stuff back and take this pack of life savers to suck on." He extended his hand toward Andy with a small pack of the small, multi-colored, candies that are packed with the emergency equipment.

"Yeah, Malik," Lieutenant Powell said. If Dawson hadn't risked his life, and had the foresight to bring some food along, we'd be getting pretty hungry about now."

"I know, Skipper. I was just playing with him. I'm going to recommend Dawson for the Distinguished Serving Cross." Everyone laughed and Powell gave him a thumb up.

"You did good Dawson," Powell said, "and I want you to know I won't forget it."

"No big deal, Captain," Dawson said. "It was better than listening to these guys' bellyaching."

"Where in hell is the navy?" Egg Money said, grumbling.

"We're pretty far out, Watson," Powell told him, "it may take a while for them to find us. I don't know how strong the battery is on the locator signal."

They passed the night without incident. The food ran out and all the empties had been tossed overboard. Early the next morning, Will was scanning the skies with the binoculars he had strapped around his neck when he left the aircraft. Most of the men were asleep.

"Aircraft, Ten O'clock low, Skipper."

Powell sat up and started looking in the direction Will was pointing. "Can you tell what it is?"

"Not yet, but it's coming this way."

"Send up a flair, Malik."

Andy retrieved a gun and cartridge from the storage pocket, loaded and fired it into the air. Shortly the aircraft drew close enough to be identified. "It's a PBY," Andy said.

Back at NAS Brunswick, the Malik family along with Andy's girlfriend, Jeanie Randall were sitting in the waiting room with Richard Dunham and Jamie Cain. They were slowly growing more despondent, having spent another night without any word of their family members who were still lost somewhere at sea.

Lieutenant Commander Jeff Woodson walked into the

room and everyone immediately looked in his direction, in hopeful anticipation.

"Folks, our guys have been found and are now aboard a Coast Guard PBY headed home. They'll be back in Brunswick in about four hours. Everybody is okay, nobody hurt."

Cheers and tears flooded the room. Jamie collapsed in her father's arms and sobbed uncontrollably. She wanted to go home and clean up and come back in time for their arrival.

"They will have to go to the base hospital to be checked out," Woodson told them. "You can see them there and stay with them until they are cleared and released."

The two families and at least two hundred base personnel and sailors from other squadrons were waiting at the hospital when the Navy bus arrived from the airfield. A loud cheer went up. The crowd cleared a path for the men of LH-12 to get into the building and for their family members to get to them.

Jamie waited as seven or eight men exited the bus before she saw Will step down. He seemed okay but all of them were moving slowly. She ran to him when he saw her and began smiling. They embraced and she began sobbing again.

"You're beautiful," he said.

"I was pretty unbeautiful until just a couple of hours ago. Dad and I spent the night at the operations building. When you didn't show up last night, I thought I was going to die. Are you okay, Darling?"

"Cold, still cold," he said.

"I was so scared. We've got to get out of this Will. If I had lost you a week before you got out, I think I would have died."

"No, you wouldn't," he said, "you would have taken care of Clare. You know you would."

"This was insanity, it was like a nightmare."

"I know, Honey, but it's all over now."

The men were kept in the hospital until the next morning just to make sure there was no hypothermia or any other physical or mental ailments. Everyone checked out and they were released. Andy Malik's mom and dad took him home for a couple of days to Lewiston and Jamie took Will home to Brunswick.

Lieutenant Powell told them he had scheduled a get together at the Officers Club the coming week for them all to say goodbye to Will.

Lieutenant Powell stood up in front of them all. The first thing he did was salute. "Gentlemen," he said. "We have an uncommon bond that will be with us the rest of our lives. As much as I regret losing our airplane, I thank God that I didn't lose any of you fine men. I believe that, had that happened, I might not have been able to continue my career in the Navy. Mister Cain will be leaving us very soon for his life on the outside and, while I would prefer that he stay onboard, I wish him the very best. I will be recommending Larry Dawson for a commendation for his foresight and fortitude in securing food for our crew while we were adrift on the sea. We'll be getting a new aircraft and some of you may be reassigned, I hope that is not the case but that is the navy way so we'll just have to wait and see what happens.

After the affair was ended, Will shook hands with each man and wished them well. He sought out Lieutenant Powell and shook hands with him. "It's been an honor serving under your command, Mister Powell," he said.

"The honor is mine, Will," Powell said, "Good luck to you. If I get out to Colorado, I will look you up."

"I hope you do, Skipper," He said, and saluted. Powell returned his salute and Will left the building and walked out to the car where Jamie was waiting for him.

CHAPTER 11

Headed West

Will Cain mustered out of the Navy in February of 1964. He thought back on the time, and on all that had happened since he first checked into the squadron. When he came here, he was all he had to worry about, now there were three of them, a wonderful wife and a little girl. His heart and his life were overflowing with more love than he ever knew existed.

At Land's End, they sat on the rocks for the last time, or at least for the last time for a long time, and he struggled for words enough to tell Jamie what he was feeling.

"I'm not very good with words," he said, but I have to tell you this. Coming to this place, so far away from everything I grew up with, and finding you here and the way things have worked out, having a daughter." He squeezed her hands in his and laughed and his laughter turned into tears and crying. "We have a daughter, Jamie. Can you believe that?"

"I know Will," she said, "we named her Clare after a café."

He laughed again and wiped the tears from his eyes. "I was listening to one of the guys a while back complaining about money. He was mad that he never has enough money. 'Why can't I ever get a break, he kept saying. He was really distraught. I've been thinking about what he said and I came to realize that I got my break. 'You're' the best break I ever got. I don't ever have to worry about 'getting a break' in life. I got my break already. I promise you this, Jamie Lynn Cain, I'll never hurt you, physically or emotionally and I'll love you till I die. I hope you'll do the same for me."

"I will, Will," she said.

"Stop it," he said and grabbed her and kissed her.

The small U-Haul trailer was attached to Will Cain's blue Ford Falcon. In the cab, a baby carrier, turned around backwards in the front seat, held a five-month old baby girl who was named after a café. Her father was at the wheel and her mother was riding shotgun. He turned onto I-95 South and started lumbering down the freeway.

"So where are we headed, Stud?" Her mother asked.

West, ma'am, we're headed West."

When I was Twenty-One

There was a time, I tell you true
O'er furrowed fields of morning dew
On Neptune wings, I fairly flew
Through skies of iridescent blue
When I was twenty-one

And there were days when, all in all
The world's demands seemed meager, small
I questioned not tomorrow's call
But that was long before the fall
When I was twenty-one

There was a time, you too must know
When a pretty face in twilight's glow
Could steal the heart and warm the soul
Ah, but that was so very long ago
When I was twenty-one

And there was a time, I used to say
When absolutes and naiveté
Were stripped and scarred
And blown away
In Dealey Plaza one November day
When I was twenty-one

And there were times, I'm not sure how
When failures life would disallow
And soft sweet hands would cool my brow
But I just can't remember now
When I was twenty-one

From "Dreams of a Forgotten Man"
By Jack Sprouse

Credits

*Postface** Information on Brunswick Naval Air Station Brunswick, Maine: Wikipedia

*Postface*** Information on Lockheed P2V Neptune Aircraft: **Military Factory** Website
http://www.militaryfactory.com/aircraft/detail.asp?aircraft_id=514

*Chapter 1** From Aviation History Magazine (Forgotten Warbird by Charles F. Clark)
*Chapter 5** Information on Roosevelt Roads Naval Air Station: Wikipedia
*Chapter 7** Information on Guantanamo Bay, Cuba CNIC Naval Station Guantanamo Bay Cuba
http://www.cnic.navy.mil/regions/cnrse/installations/ns_guantanamo_bay.html
Wikipedia   http://en.wikipedia.org/wiki/Guant%C3%A1namo_Bay
*Chapter 7*** Russian ships during the Cuban Missile Crises
http://www.history.navy.mil/faqs/faq90-5c.htm
*Chapter 8** Information on the Azores Islands: Wikipedia
*Chapter 8*** Picture of two VP-21 Neptunes passing Gibraltar in 1963
http://www.verslo.is/baldur/p2/vp21.htm

The Author, Sicily 1963

POSTFACE

Brunswick Naval Air Station, designated NAS Brunswick, or 'Broomstick' as the squadron crews referred to it was located just outside of Brunswick, Maine. The base was originally built and occupied in March of 1943 and fully commissioned in April of 1945. Its first use was to accommodate Royal Navy Air elements of the British Naval Command.

The land on which the base was built was donated by the town of Brunswick which had been using it for a small municipal airport. The first US Navy squadron to arrive at NAS Brunswick was VS 1D1, a scouting squadron that, along with units of the Royal Navy Air Arms used the base to engage in around the clock anti-submarine warfare (ASW) missions off the East coast. The base was deactivated in 1946 but then reactivated in 1951 as a fully operational Naval Air Station. *Preface* credits*

Lockheed P2V Neptune

The P2V Neptune series of aircraft was one of the more successful post-war designs for America, with service that spanned decades for a handful of America-friendly countries. The system was designed by Lockheed Corporation as a land-based maritime patrol and reconnaissance platform. The system proved so versatile and effective that the base production model spawned a large series of variants in specialized roles.

The P2V Neptune was a twin engine high-wing monoplane design. Sporting various Wright-brand Power Plants throughout its production run the aircraft featured outstanding range.

The Neptune got its start as early as 1944. Initial models featured an impressive armament cannons and heavy caliber machine guns of which 6 x20 mm cannons were mounted in a battery in the nose while 2 x 20 mm cannons sat in tail turret. 2 x 12.7 mm machine guns were also part of the early arsenal. Many of these weapons were later removed as the mission changed. For a time the aircraft had the ability to carry torpedoes, mines, bombs of various weights and even under the wing high explosive rockets.

Specifications:

Initial year of service: 1947, Production: 1,036
Length: 77ft
Width: 100ft
Height: 27.99ft
Weight (Empty): 41,548lbs
Weight (MTOW): 79,999lbs
Power plant: 2 x Weight R-3350-30W 1-stage-2-speed supercharged piston engines generating 3,250 hp each
Maximum Speed: 314 mph
Maximum Range: 2,807 miles
Service Ceiling: 24,698ft
Rate-of-Climb: 1,100 feet per minute

Armament Suite:

6 x 100lb bombs
6 x 500lb bombs
4 x 1,000lb bombs
2 x 2,000lb mines
2 x 1,600lb mines
4 x Mk 24 mines
4 x Mk 34 mines
2 x A. R. 11.75 inch
16 x HVAR 5 inch rockets (underwing)

Variants:

XP2V-1: Prototype Model Designation of which two examples were ordered in 1944

P2V-1: Initial Production Model Designation

P2V-2: Removed nose turret and extended nose

P2V-2S: Specialized ASW Variant

P2V-2N: Specialized Artic Variant with skis

P2V-3: Improved Engines

P2V-3C: Improved Carrier Variant

P2V-3Z: Command Transport Variant

P2V-3W: Early Warning Radar Search Variant

P2V-4: Fitted with Turbo Compound R 3350 engines, standard APS-20 radar, and wingtip fuel tanks

P2V-5: First version offered for export

P2V-6: Reduced capability radar, improved defensive armament positions

P2V-7: Final Production Model, fitted with Westinghouse J-34 wingtip pods, tail turret replaced by MAD boom system, nose armament removed, redesigned cockpit

SP2H: New designation replaced previous P2V designations

The aircraft flown by VP-21 in the 1960s carried no weapons. The nose cannons had been removed and the nose of the aircraft extended to incorporate an observation station. The compartment was protected by a Plexiglas cover and a chair on runners that allowed the observer to extend himself into the bubble and easily see on all sides with no line of sight impediment. The tail turret was removed to make room for the MAD (Magnetic Anomaly Detector) gear. The aircraft designation changed to SP-2H after 1962 but it was still referred to as the P2V by most of the Neptune crews. *Postface**credits*

About the Author
Jack Sprouse

Hometown: Dallas, Texas, although I now live in Lewisville, a few miles north of Dallas.

I studied American History at Texas Tech, in Lubbock, and my fields of greatest historical interest are The American Civil War and World War II.

I served in the United States Navy as a crewmember on an ASW (Anti-Submarine-Warfare) patrol aircraft.

Writing fiction is my passion. I just love making stuff up (my mom used to punish me for doing that when I was a kid).

I have written two books of historical fiction (Adventures in Time Book I, The American Civil War. and Book II, Adventures in Time, The American West. These are both Walter Mitty type stories in which I place myself back in time as a war correspondent following historical events and interviewing the major players in those events.

Two books of original poetry: *The Quiet Place & Dreams of a Forgotten Man*. Both books contain approx. 50 original poems on various subjects: Life, love, friendship, relationships, war, conflict, tragedy.

Seven of my novels have been published by Black Opal Books, in Oregon
> Clare
> Magnolia Road
> Dreams Once Dreamed
> A Bowl Full of Grapes
> The House Wren
> False River
> On Neptune Wings

I am currently working on a couple of new books which I expect will keep me busy for the next five or six months.